Truth & Lies

Truth&Lies

AN ANTHOLOGY OF POEMS

EDITED BY
PATRICE VECCHIONE

HENRY HOLT AND COMPANY • NEW YORK

For my goddaughter Kyle Van West
and for my nephews Nicholas Gardner
and Joshua Gardner

Henry Holt and Company, LLC
Publishers since 1866
115 West 18th Street
New York, New York 10011

Henry Holt is a registered trademark of Henry Holt and Company, LLC

Published in Canada by Fitzhenry & Whiteside Ltd.,
195 Allstate Parkway, Markham, Ontario L3R 4T8.

Library of Congress Cataloging-in-Publication Data
Truth and lies: an anthology of poems / edited by Patrice Vecchione.
       p.   cm.
    Includes index.
    1. Children's poetry.   2. Truthfulness and falsehood—Juvenile poetry.
    [1. Truthfulness and falsehood—Poetry.   2. Poetry—Collections.]
    I. Vecchione, Patrice.
    PN6109.97 .T78   2000   808.81'0083—dc21   00-38871

ISBN 0-8050-6479-6
First Edition—2001
Printed in the United States of America on acid-free paper. ∞

10   9   8   7   6   5   4   3   2   1

I wanted to live in accord with the promptings which came from my true self. Why is that so very difficult?

—Herman Hesse

ACKNOWLEDGMENTS

Many thanks to my editor Marc Aronson for his vision, keen eye, and ear; to Leslie Auerbach for helping to winnow and form; to Joëlle Dujardin, whose reliable assistance I came to count on; to Alyssa Raymond, who sniffed out several poems that I can't imagine this book without; to Charlotte Raymond, who negotiates more than contracts; to Michael Heim, for his help; to Don Rothman, innovative thinker and generous friend; to the Seaside High School students and their teacher Cheryl Joseph, who listened to a number of these poems and wrote in response to them; to sleuth Marion Silverbear, not only for her assistance, which went far beyond writing letters and looking for poems and poets, but also for her good humor and the time she called a publisher only to find out that she had dialed the number for the Chinese Kitchen so that we nearly ordered takeout; to Michael Stark, his patience and indulgences; to the poets who give this book its truth.

Thank you also to the reference departments at both the Monterey City Library and the Santa Cruz County Library, particularly to Victor H. Bausch, Doug Holtzman, and Steve Parker; to Gā Lombard of Bookshop Santa Cruz; Connie Tanada and Consul Nontshukumo Phama of the South African Consulate; Janet Greenberg, Mercedes Roffe, Deborah Turner, Nick Vecchione, Ken Weisner, and Diana Wertz, who searched and found.

CONTENTS

On Truth, Lies, and Poetry | | xiii
From The Simple Truth | *Philip Levine* | 3
Brotherhood | *Octavio Paz* | 4
The Unwritten | *W. S. Merwin* | 5
The Secret | *Denise Levertov* | 7
Song of the Bald Eagle | *The Crow People* | 9
When We Were Here Together | *Kenneth Patchen* | 10
Remember | *Joy Harjo* | 12
From 33 | *Julia Alvarez* | 13
why some people be mad at me
    sometimes | *Lucille Clifton* | 14
Lies | *Yevgeny Yevtushenko* | 15
"The teachers taught her that the
    world was round" | *Gertrude Stein* | 16
Horse's Head | *Jonell Hill* | 17
The Old Man Said: One | *Gogisgi/Carroll Arnett* | 20
Truth and Falsehood | *Robert Herrick* | 21
Truth | *Robert Herrick* | 22
We Have Been Believers | *Margaret Walker* | 23
True Stories | *Margaret Atwood* | 25
The Wayfarer | *Stephen Crane* | 27
Our Principal | *Naomi Shihab Nye* | 28
Therefore I Must Tell the Truth | *Torlino* | 29
Beat | *Janet S. Wong* | 30
A Song of Lies on Sabbath Eve | *Yehuda Amichai* | 31
The Stincher | *Jackie Kay* | 32
From Caught | *Rodney Jones* | 34

A Poison Tree	*William Blake*	35
From A Shadow Play for Guilt	*Marge Piercy*	36
what goes around comes around		
or the proof is in the pudding	*Cheryl Clarke*	37
Our Lies and Their Beauty	*Bruce Weigl*	38
Tell All the Truth	*Emily Dickinson*	40
Mirror	*Sylvia Plath*	41
Four Masks	*Cortney Davis*	42
From To Julia de Burgos	*Julia de Burgos*	44
I Am Not I	*Juan Ramón Jiménez*	46
Sure You Can Ask Me a Personal		
Question	*Diane Burns*	47
Be Like Others	*Czeslaw Milosz*	49
Denial	*Kinereth Gensler*	51
Don't Tell a Soul	*Osip Mandelstam*	52
The Other Voices	*Linda Hogan*	53
In My Country	*Pitika Ntuli*	55
The Democratic Judge	*Bertolt Brecht*	56
The Body Politic	*Donald Hall*	58
Small Heart	*Zbigniew Herbert*	59
Bilingual Sestina	*Julia Alvarez*	61
Smoke and Deception	*Raymond Carver*	63
From Cartographies of Silence	*Adrienne Rich*	64
"When my love swears that she is		
made of truth"	*William Shakespeare*	66
From Fragment 26	*Sappho*	67
crush	*Rita Wong*	68
Appeal	*Edith Nesbit*	69
A Renewal	*James Merrill*	70
How She Resolved to Act	*Merrill Moore*	71
With the Door Open	*David Ignatow*	72
A Secret Kept	*Judah al-Harizi*	73
Hiding Our Love	*Carolyn Kizer*	74

"And the days are not full enough"   *Ezra Pound*   75
I Am Asking You to Come Back Home   *Jo Carson*   76
Hypocrisy   *Samuel Butler*   78
Sous-Entendu   *Anne Stevenson*   79
The Lie   *Sir Walter Ralegh*   80
Come All You Fair and Tender Ladies *Anonymous*   84
Song   *Sir George Etherege*   85
The Fool's Song   *William Carlos Williams* 86
To a Friend Whose Work Has Come
    to Nothing   *W. B. Yeats*   87
The Clay Jug   *Kabir*   88
A Box Called the Imagination   *Zbigniew Herbert*   89
The Girl Who Became My
    Grandmother   *Morton Marcus*   91
The Way Through the Woods   *Rudyard Kipling*   93
Not Forever on Earth   *King Nezahualcoyotl*   94
no help for that   *Charles Bukowski*   95

Biographical Notes   97
Permissions   133
Index of Authors   139
Index of Titles   141

ON TRUTH, LIES, AND POETRY

How do you know what's true and what isn't? Can you distinguish an honest kiss from one that isn't? You believe it is love until your heart is broken and you know you have been duped. As we make decisions for our lives, we have to decide who we can trust, when we are secure, and with whom. Is it the way a person looks at you, the telepathic attention of the loved one's eyes? Does it have to do with how carefully someone listens, or is it that they show up when they say they will?

TRUTH

> *The truth isn't always beauty but the hunger for it is.*
>
> —Nadine Gordimer

Basic truths such as the need for love, the comfort of understanding, the necessity to stand up for what we believe in are at the heart of being human. Sometimes a thing is so true it's as though it's been spoken even when it hasn't. Truth can find us when we're lost. And yet there are the truths you wish you never knew, would like to forget. Often there isn't just one truth, there are many. What's most true right now might not be so later. Then there are some truths so true that if you really accepted them, you'd have to change your life.

LIES

you know that the saddest lies
are the ones we tell ourselves.

—Lucille Clifton

A lie can be spoken, but it can also be what is left out of a conversation. People's actions can lie, making what they say complete illusion. Lies can be used to hurt, manipulate, or to protect. Some say that even the little "white lies" we tell do more to shelter the speaker than the one being spoken to. If you go along with something you know is untrue, are you contributing to that lie? But what is the price of telling the truth? Sometimes it can cost you your friends, your family, even your country. Is that too high a price?

At times we need to keep what we feel a secret for a while. Even recognizing that is a truth. We may hide what we feel in order to take care of ourselves, to lick our wounds. A friend asks, "How are you doing?" Maybe it's even the friend who only hours ago insulted you, and there's no way you want to reveal your true feeling, so you answer, "Fine, just fine," when really you're not fine at all. You bite the inside of your cheek just to be able to give the answer that lets you hide. Or we lie when we know the truth could endanger not only our psyches but our skins. What kind of lying is that? We might call it survival.

POETRY

Inside this pencil
crouch words that have never been written

never been spoken
never been thought

they're hiding

—W. S. Merwin

Poetry is a particular way of telling the truth. Poems can uncover things. Often a poem will say what you know is true but had never heard put into words before. Facts are only the hard edges of things; poems twist and turn the facts in order to get to what's inside them. Poets may lie in order to get to the truth. A poem doesn't enter through the front door. It goes in the back or through a window. A poem leads you into a familiar room, now filled with something strange, and you wonder how it got there, but it's true and right, and now you know it, too. A poem can be a quiet and private kind of telling. Other poems shout to us from the page; they're declarations, loud and insistent. We stop what we're doing to listen. Some poems are like prayers; they tell us what we hope is true, and we may say them over and over, trying to bring their message nearer to our lives.

How does a poem make us fall for it? When I read poetry, there's a three-punch response I'm after—first in my body, then an emotional response. I want it to cause me to feel in a way I couldn't have anticipated. Finally, I want the poem to give me things to think about. If I put the poem down, grab a soda from the fridge, or take my bike out for a spin, and the poem stays with me, I'm hooked. It may only spend an hour in my thoughts, or it may enter my dreams, but, even in some small way, I'm changed by what I've read.

For this collection, I looked for poems to say things in new ways, poems that could wake a reader up. I chose poetry that would make one give up any resistance; poems that are reminders of the force and strength of human spirit and dignity and of the impulse to speak and make art out of life. The poems demonstrate the hunger for what is true, even when it costs us. Some show what happens when we've lost our way from the truth, the moral and political implications of honesty or the lack of it, the rippling effect that lies can have, how to cope with the ones we've told, and how to live with our mistakes.

In deciding on an order for the poems that make up *Truth and Lies*, I knew I wanted it to be organic, not as in a vegetable but as in authentic. The Crow people's "Song of the Bald Eagle" says, "We want what is real," and that's what I wanted for this book. I'd just written my first draft of the introduction, having given a lot of thought to the connections among truth, lies, and poetry, when I found Philip Levine's poem "The Simple Truth" and it aligned perfectly with what I was thinking about. *There's the book's beginning*, I thought. Let's start with what we know and show how some truths are simple and elegant and that they belong to us. Then I wanted to give support for that foundation. What holds our truths up; just what do we know and what can we trust? Ultimately, as Octavio Paz says, this is what we know: ". . . little do I last / and the night is enormous. . . ." Yet we are connected to that night. A poem lets you in on the way the writer sees things, and that can be like sharing a secret. Denise Levertov's poem "The Secret" describes how a reader may bring a truth to the poem and find something that the author didn't know was there.

In my living room, the poems were spread on the floor for days. My fiancé was kind about having to go through the back door and keep the windows shut. I was sprawled on the floor, muttering to myself, as I found alliances I hadn't seen before between poems. I knew Zbigniew Herbert's poem "Small Heart" had to go with Donald Hall's "The Body Politic" the moment I found Hall's poem in my local library one afternoon. Others in the library knew that, too, because I kind of yelped a rather nonlibrary yelp when I made my discovery. In both the Herbert and Hall poems, a narrator has painful consequences to live with, two sides of a many-sided experience. But unearthing the connection between the Rodney Jones poem "Caught" and William Blake's "A Poison Tree" wasn't in my original plan. I found the link as I read the works over and over again. I like the way Sappho's verse from Fragment 26, written more than two thousand years ago, sits next to Rita Wong's "crush," written recently, and how both poems speak to what it's like to be hurt by life, to be lied to.

I wanted to arrange the poems delicately so that a reader could enter the experience of what it's like to be deceived, and stay there for a while, but then move on to other aspects of honesty and dishonesty. The theme of truth and lies in love, for instance, isn't stuck in just one place in this book but appears, disappears, and then comes back just as truth and lies do in life. Throughout this book, the poems ask us to question what we know for certain.

But don't take my word for it. Find the poems that

speak to you. What do you find true? Are you persuaded to believe? Poems can be as messy, complex, and immoral as our actions toward one another. They are no more real than we are. Or maybe they are; maybe they make manifest ultimate and divine truths, and that's what makes poetry art. Speak back to these works. Bring your questions with you when you turn the page. Make the poems stand up. Then pick up a pen and grab a sheaf of paper. If you don't speak your own truth, who will?

—Patrice Vecchione

Truth&Lies

from THE SIMPLE TRUTH

>   . . . Some things
> you know all your life. They are so simple and true
> they must be said without elegance, meter and rhyme,
> they must be laid on the table beside the salt shaker,
> the glass of water, the absence of light gathering
> in the shadows of the picture frames, they must be
> naked and alone, they must stand for themselves. . . .

PHILIP LEVINE

BROTHERHOOD

Homage to Claudius Ptolemy

I am a man: little do I last
and the night is enormous.
But I look up:
the stars write.
Unknowingly I understand:
I too am written,
and at this very moment
someone spells me out.

OCTAVIO PAZ

THE UNWRITTEN

Inside this pencil
crouch words that have never been written
never been spoken
never been thought

they're hiding

they're awake in there
dark in the dark
hearing us
but they won't come out
not for love not for time not for fire

even when the dark has worn away
they'll still be there
hiding in the air
multitudes in days to come may walk through them
breathe them
be none the wiser

what script can it be
that they won't unroll
in what language
would I recognize it
would I be able to follow it
to make out the real names
of everything

maybe there aren't
many
it could be that there's only one word
and it's all we need
it's here in this pencil

every pencil in the world
is like this

W. S. MERWIN

THE SECRET

Two girls discover
the secret of life
in a sudden line of
poetry.

I who don't know the
secret wrote
the line. They
told me

(through a third person)
they had found it
but not what it was
not even

what line it was. No doubt
by now, more than a week
later, they have forgotten
the secret,

the line, the name of
the poem. I love them
for finding what
I can't find,

and for loving me
for the line I wrote,
and for forgetting it
so that

a thousand times, till death
finds them, they may
discover it again, in other
lines

in other
happenings. And for
wanting to know it,
for

assuming there is
such a secret, yes,
for that
most of all.

DENISE LEVERTOV

SONG OF THE BALD EAGLE

we want what is real
we want what is real
don't deceive us!

TRADITIONAL SONG OF THE CROW PEOPLE

WHEN WE WERE HERE TOGETHER

When we were here together in a place we did not know, nor one another.

A bit of grass held between the teeth for a moment, bright hair on the wind. What we were we did not know, nor ever the grass or the flame of hair turning to ash on the wind.

But they lied about that. From the beginning they lied. To the child, telling him that there was somewhere anger against him, and a hatred against him, and only for the reason of his being in the world. But never did they tell him that the only evil and danger was in themselves; that they alone were the poisoners and the betrayers; that they—they *alone*—were responsible for what was being done in the world.

And they told the child to starve and to kill the child that was within him; for only by doing this could he safely enter their world; only by doing this could he become a useful and adjusted member of the community which they had prepared for him. And this time, alas, they did not lie.

And with the death of the child was born a thing that had neither the character of a man nor the character of a child, but was a horrible and monstrous parody of the two; and it is in his world now the flesh of man's spirit lies twisted and despoiled under the indifferent stars.

When we were here together in a place we did not know, nor one another. O green this bit of warm grass between our teeth—O beautiful the hair of our mortal goddess on the indifferent wind.

KENNETH PATCHEN

REMEMBER

Remember the sky you were born under,
know each of the star's stories.
Remember the moon, know who she is.
Remember the sun's birth at dawn, that is the
strongest point of time. Remember sundown
and the giving away to night.
Remember your birth, how your mother struggled
to give you form and breath. You are evidence of
her life, and her mother's, and hers.
Remember your father. He is your life, also.
Remember the earth whose skin you are:
red earth, black earth, yellow earth, white earth
brown earth, we are earth.
Remember the plants, trees, animal life who all have
their tribes, their families, their histories, too. Talk to
them, listen to them. They are alive poems.
Remember the wind. Remember her voice. She
knows the origin of this universe.
Remember you are all people and that all people
are you.
Remember you are the universe and this
universe is you.
Remember all is in motion, is growing, is you.
Remember language comes from this.
Remember the dance language is, that life is.
Remember.

JOY HARJO

from 33

Sometimes the words are so close I am
more who I am when I'm down on paper
than anywhere else as if my life were
practising for the real me I become
unbuttoned from the anecdotal and
unnecessary and undressed down
to the figure of the poem, line by line,
the real text a child could understand.
Why do I get confused living it through?
Those of you, lost and yearning to be free,
who hear these words, take heart from me.
I once was in as many drafts as you.
But briefly, essentially, here I am . . .
Who touches this poem touches a woman.

JULIA ALVAREZ

WHY SOME PEOPLE BE MAD
AT ME SOMETIMES

they ask me to remember
but they want me to remember
their memories
and i keep on remembering
mine.

LUCILLE CLIFTON

LIES

Telling lies to the young is wrong.
Proving to them that lies are true is wrong.
Telling them that God's in his heaven
and all's well with the world is wrong.
The young know what you mean. The young are
people.
Tell them the difficulties can't be counted,
and let them see not only what will be
but see with clarity these present times.
Say obstacles exist they must encounter
sorrow happens, hardship happens.
The hell with it. Who never knew
the price of happiness will not be happy.
Forgive no error you recognize,
it will repeat itself, increase,
and afterwards our pupils
will not forgive in us what we forgave.

YEVGENY YEVTUSHENKO

THE TEACHERS TAUGHT HER THAT THE WORLD WAS ROUND

The teachers taught her
That the world was round
That the sun was round
That the moon was round
That the stars were round
And that they were all going around and around
And not a sound.
It was sad it almost made her cry
But then she did not believe it
Because the mountains were so high,
And so she thought she had better sing
And then a dreadful thing was happening
She remembered when she had been young
That one day she had sung,
And there was a looking glass in front of her
And as she sang her mouth was round and was going
    around and around.
Oh dear oh dear was everything just to be round and
    go around and around.
What could she do but try and remember the
    mountains were so high they could stop anything.
But she could not keep on remembering and forgetting
    of course not but she could sing of course she could
    sing and she could cry of course she could cry.
Oh my.

GERTRUDE STEIN

HORSE'S HEAD

When first you see it you cannot say it,
and when you do say it
it stutters from your mouth
in a terrible Morse-Code
that no-one can decipher.
Your brothers smirk, your father stares,
your mother offers remedial mugs
of hot milk, the promise of bed,

but you stand resolute,
trembling, stupidly mute until,
reluctantly they follow you back
into the icy dusk.

You need them to know what you cannot tell

how you stumbled there,
how it blazed
startling and white
as a meteor
beneath the black water,
the flannelled nostrils, the lashes,
the pleats of the muzzle
already rimmed with an etching of algae.
And the single eye, wide open
staring
up at you, the jaw
clenched tight . . .

Walking through the snow
you pass your own footprints
slurry in the setting sun and running
in the opposite direction,
and you know then
it will be too late,
that the thin skin of evening ice
will seal away the secret
that no one else will see.

Already your father stands bellowing
at the edge of the pond, his breath hanging
hot against the freezing air,
yelling

> *There is nothing! Nothing there!*
> *And what kind of person would do that sort of*
>   *thing?*
> *What kind of person would hack off a horse's*
>   *head*
> *and throw it in a pond?! Tell me! What kind*
>   *of person?!*

And you want to tell him

It is the kind of person
that held the hunting knife against
your own white throat
and made you promise never to speak

of the other things he had done
and would do
and would not stop.

JONELL HILL

THE OLD MAN SAID: ONE

Some will tell
you it doesn't
matter. That is
a lie. Everything,
every single thing
matters. And
nothing good
happens fast.

GOGISGI/CARROLL ARNETT

TRUTH AND FALSEHOOD

Truth by her own simplicity is known,
Falsehood by varnish and vermillion.

ROBERT HERRICK

TRUTH

Truth is best found out by the time, and eyes;
Falsehood winnes credit by uncertainties.

ROBERT HERRICK

WE HAVE BEEN BELIEVERS

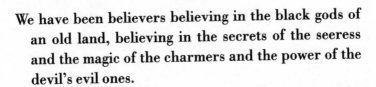

We have been believers believing in the black gods of
an old land, believing in the secrets of the seeress
and the magic of the charmers and the power of the
devil's evil ones.

And in the white gods of a new land we have been
believers believing in the mercy of our masters and
the beauty of our brothers, believing in the conjure
of the humble and the faithful and the pure.

Neither the slaves' whip nor the lynchers' rope nor the
bayonet could kill our black belief. In our hunger
we beheld the welcome table and in our nakedness
the glory of a long white robe. We have been believ-
ers in the new Jerusalem.

We have been believers feeding greedy grinning gods,
like a Moloch demanding our sons and our daugh-
ters, our strength and our wills and our spirits of
pain. We have been believers, silent and stolid and
stubborn and strong.

We have been believers yielding substance for the
world. With our hands have we fed a people and out
of our strength have they wrung the necessities of a
nation. Our song has filled the twilight and our
hope has heralded the dawn.

Now we stand ready for the touch of one fiery iron, for
the cleansing breath of many molten truths, that the

eyes of the blind may see and the ears of the deaf may hear and the tongues of the people be filled with living fire.

Where are our gods that they leave us asleep? Surely the priests and the preachers and the powers will hear. Surely now that our hands are empty and our hearts too full to pray they will understand. Surely the sires of the people will send us a sign.

We have been believers believing in our burdens and our demigods too long. Now the needy no longer weep and pray; the long-suffering arise, and our fists bleed against the bars with a strange insistency.

MARGARET WALKER

TRUE STORIES

i

Don't ask for the true story;
why do you need it?

It's not what I set out with
or what I carry.

What I'm sailing with,
a knife, blue fire,

luck, a few good words
that still work, and the tide.

ii

The true story was lost
on the way down to the beach, it's something

I never had, that black tangle
of branches in a shifting light,

my blurred footprints
filling with salt

water, this handful
of tiny bones, this owl's kill;

a moon, crumpled papers, a coin,
the glint of an old picnic,

the hollows made by lovers
in sand a hundred

years ago: no clue.

iii

The true story lies
among the other stories,

a mess of colors, like jumbled clothing
thrown off or away,

like hearts on marble, like syllables, like
butchers' discards.

The true story is vicious
and multiple and untrue

after all. Why do you
need it? Don't ever

ask for the true story.

MARGARET ATWOOD

THE WAYFARER

The wayfarer,
Perceiving the pathway to truth,
Was struck with astonishment.
It was thickly grown with weeds.
"Ha," he said,
"I see that no one has passed here
In a long time."
Later he saw that each weed
Was a singular knife.
"Well," he mumbled at last,
"Doubtless there are other roads."

STEPHEN CRANE

OUR PRINCIPAL

beat his wife.
We did not know it then.
We knew his slanted-stripe
ties.
We said, "Good morning"
in our cleanest voices.
He stood beside the door
of the office
where all our unborn
report cards lived.
He had twins
and reddish hair.
Later the news
would seep
along the gutters,
chilly stream
of autumn rain.
My mother,
newspaper dropped down
on the couch, staring
out the window—
All those years I told you
pay good attention to
what he says.

NAOMI SHIHAB NYE

28

THEREFORE I MUST TELL THE TRUTH

I am ashamed before the earth:
I am ashamed before the heavens:
I am ashamed before the dawn:
I am ashamed before the evening twilight:
I am ashamed before the blue sky:
I am ashamed before the darkness:
I am ashamed before the sun:
*I am ashamed before that standing within me which
    speaks with me:*
Some of these things are always looking at me.
I am never out of sight.
Therefore I must tell the truth.
That is why I always tell the truth.
I hold my word tight to my breast.

TORLINO

BEAT

When I was small
they spanked me with a newspaper
rolled tight,
and I would yell
until the neighbors
opened their warped
wooden windows.

Now they have learned
a better way,
and the pain hurts worse
than a whipping
when they shake
their heads, whispering,
"We are so ashamed,"
in a room so quiet
you hear them
swallow.

JANET S. WONG

A SONG OF LIES ON SABBATH EVE

On a Sabbath eve, at dusk on a summer day
when I was a child,
when the odors of food and prayer drifted up from all
the houses
and the wings of the Sabbath angels rustled in the air,
I began to lie to my father:
"I went to another synagogue."

I don't know if he believed me or not
but the lie was very sweet in my mouth.
And in all the houses at night
hymns and lies drifted up together,
O taste and see,
and in all the houses at night
Sabbath angels died like flies in the lamp,
and lovers put mouth to mouth
and inflated one another till they floated in the air
or burst.

Since then, lying has tasted very sweet to me,
and since then I've always gone to another synagogue.
And my father returned the lie when he died:
"I've gone to another life."

YEHUDA AMICHAI

THE STINCHER

When I was three, I told a lie.
To this day that lie is a worry.

Some lies are too big to swallow;
some lies so gigantic they grow

in the dark, ballooning and blossoming;
some lies tell lies and flower,

hyacinths; some develop extra tongues,
purple and thick. This lie went wrong.

I told my parents my brother drowned.
I watched my mother chase my brother's name,

saw her comb the banks with her fingers
down by the river Stincher.

I chucked a stone into the deep brown water,
drowned it in laughter; my father, puffing,

found my brother's fishing reel and stool
down by the river Stincher.

I believed in the word disaster.
Lies make things happen, swell, seed, swarm.

Years from that away-from-home lie,
I don't know why I made my brother die.

I shrug my shoulders, when asked, raise my
eyebrows: *I don't know, right, I was three.*

Now I'm thirty-three. That day they rushed me
to the family friends' where my brother sat

undrowned, not frothing at the mouth, sat
innocent, quiet, watching the colourful TV.

Outside, the big mouth of the river Stincher
pursed its lips, sulked and ran away.

JACKIE KAY

from CAUGHT

There is in the human voice
A quavery vowel sometimes,
More animal than meaning,
More mineral than gentle,

A slight nuance by which my
Mother would recognize lies,
Detect scorn or envy, sober
Things words would not admit,

Though it's true the best liars
Must never know they lie
They move among good-byes
Worded like congratulations

We listen for and hear until
Some misery draws us back
To what it really was they
Obviously meant not to say . . .

RODNEY JONES

A POISON TREE

I was angry with my friend:
I told my wrath, my wrath did end.
I was angry with my foe:
I told it not, my wrath did grow.

And I watered it in fears,
Night and morning with my tears;
And I sunnèd it with smiles,
And with soft deceitful wiles.

And it grew both day and night
Till it bore an apple bright;
And my foe beheld it shine,
And he knew that it was mine,

And into my garden stole
When the night had veiled the pole:
In the morning glad I see
My foe outstretched beneath the tree.

WILLIAM BLAKE

from A SHADOW PLAY FOR GUILT

A man can lie to himself.
A man can lie with his tongue
and his brain and his gestures;
a man can lie with his life.
But the body cannot lie.

You want to take your good body off like a glove.
You want to stretch it and shrink it
as you change your abstractions.

You stand in the flesh with shame.
You smell your fingers and lick your disgust
and are satisfied.
But the beaten dog of the body remembers.

MARGE PIERCY

WHAT GOES AROUND COMES AROUND OR THE PROOF IS IN THE PUDDING

Truthfulness, honor, is not something which springs ablaze of itself: it has to be created between people . . .
                              —Adrienne Rich, "Women and Honor"

A woman in my shower crying.
All I can do is make potato salad
and wish I hadn't been caught lying.

I dust the chicken for frying
pretending my real feelings too much a challenge
to the woman in my shower crying.

I forget to boil the eggs, time is flying,
my feet are tired, my nerves frazzled,
and I wish I hadn't been caught lying.

Secondary relationships are trying.
I'd rather roll dough than be hassled
by women in my shower crying.

Truth is clarifying.
Pity it's not more like butter.
I wish I hadn't been caught lying.

Ain't no point denying,
my soufflé won't even flutter.
I withhold from the woman in my shower crying
afraid of the void I filled with lying.

CHERYL CLARKE

OUR LIES AND THEIR BEAUTY

I have loved most
the incongruous
the wildly pointless,

the oddly non-self
aggrandizing;
how one sweet man

whose mouth I would still kiss,
lied to me
that his ne'er-do-well father

stood once,
alone out on a thin steel beam
dangled

twenty stories
above the teeming city
by a nervous crane.

The man that he lied was his father
wears a white muscle t-shirt
in the photograph,

his black hair is curly
and tangled
nicely in that high city wind.

His legs spread like a dog's,
his fists
poised on his defiant hips,

he smiles a fearlessness
that you want to but
can't quite believe.

One sad night
my friend showed me
a bent-up photograph

of this man on a beam,
and I did not tell him
how I'd seen it on postcards

many times before.
It could have been his father.
They were just then building the Waldorf.

My friend lied
because he wanted his father
to be the man up there in his lie,

and because he wanted to weave something
frightened that he saw inside of me
with something

that he saw inside of himself,
the beauty
that must never always be the lie.

BRUCE WEIGL

TELL ALL THE TRUTH

Tell all the Truth but tell it slant—
Success in Circuit lies
Too bright for our infirm Delight
The Truth's superb surprise;
As Lightning to the Children eased
With explanation kind,
The Truth must dazzle gradually
Or every man be blind—

EMILY DICKINSON

MIRROR

I am silver and exact. I have no preconceptions.
Whatever I see I swallow immediately
Just as it is, unmisted by love or dislike.
I am not cruel, only truthful—
The eye of a little god, four-cornered.
Most of the time I meditate on the opposite wall.
It is pink with speckles. I have looked at it so long
I think it is a part of my heart. But it flickers.
Faces and darkness separate us over and over.

Now I am a lake. A woman bends over me.
Searching my reaches for what she really is.
Then she turns to those liars, the candles or the
    moon.
I see her back, and reflect it faithfully.
She rewards me with tears and an agitation of hands.
I am important to her. She comes and goes.
Each morning it is her face that replaces the
    darkness.
In me she has drowned a young girl, and in me an old
    woman
Rises toward her day after day, like a terrible fish.

SYLVIA PLATH

FOUR MASKS

The mask I see in the mirror:

A woman who has come to love silence,
who sees life through prisms, hexagonal
planes like the vision
of flying insects, so much color
breaking against reason. Thin
eyebrows. Nose off center.

The mask I wore for my mother:

Bright in the way of silk roses,
more than once it threw dinner
crashing to the floor and yet
was afraid to disobey.
At night it stood at the top of the long stairs
just to hear her talking.

The mask I swore my mother wore:

Small clouds like lace
on the brow. Eyepieces
I couldn't see through.
Even her small shoulders
would make me cry. When she died
I saw her face.

The mask I passed on to my children:

Comes late for dinner
and leaves early, clears the dishes quickly.
This mask
is all relatives alive or dead,
drunk, sober, or beautiful. Oh God, yes,
at least beautiful.
Everyone at the table finds a window,
stares intently through.

CORTNEY DAVIS

from **TO JULIA DE BURGOS**

Already the people murmur that I am your enemy,
that in poetry I give you the world.

They lie, Julia de Burgos. They lie, Julia de Burgos.
What rises in my verses is not your voice: it's my voice
because you are the clothes and I am the essence;
between us extends the most profound abyss.

You are the cold doll of social lies,
and I, the virile glimmer of human truth.

You are the honey of gentle hypocrisies; not I;
in all my poems I bare my heart.

You, like your world, are selfish; not I;
I gamble everything to be what I am.

You are only the haughty lady, señorona;*
not I; I am life, strength, woman.

You belong to your husband, your master; not I;
I belong to nobody, or to all, to all, to all
I give myself in my clean feelings and thoughts.

You curl your hair and paint your face; not I;
I am curled by the wind and painted by the sun.

*Señorona implies a woman who is high and mighty, "a great lady."

You are the lady of the house, resigned, submissive,
tied to the bigotry of men; not I;
I am an unbridled workhorse running
snorting the horizons of God's justice . . .

JULIA DE BURGOS

I AM NOT I

I am not I.
                  I am this one
walking beside me, the one I cannot see;
the one I sometimes see
and at other times forget,
who is silent and calm when I speak,
the one who forgives, sweetly, when I hate,
who walks where I am not,
the one who will remain standing when I die.

JUAN RAMÓN JIMÉNEZ

SURE YOU CAN ASK ME A PERSONAL QUESTION

How do you do?
No, I'm not Chinese.
No, not Spanish.
No, I'm American Indi—uh, Native American.
No, not from India.
No, we're not extinct.
No, not Navajo.
No, not Sioux.
Yes, Indian.
Oh, so you've had an Indian friend?
            That close.
Oh, so you've had an Indian lover?
            That tight.
Oh, so you've had an Indian servant?
            That much.
Oh, so that's where you got those high cheekbones.
Your great-grandmother, eh?
Hair down to there?
Let me guess—Cherokee?
Oh, an Indian Princess.
No, I didn't make it rain tonight.
No, I don't know where you can get Navajo rugs real
    cheap.
No, I don't know where you can get peyote.
No, I didn't make this—I bought it at
    Bloomingdale's.
Yes, some of us drink too much.

Some of us can't drink enuf.
This ain't no stoic look.
This is my face.

DIANE BURNS

BE LIKE OTHERS

Wherever you lived—in the city of Pergamum at the time of the Emperor Hadrian, in Marseilles under Louis XV or in the New Amsterdam of the colonists— be aware that you should consider yourself lucky if your life followed the pattern of your neighbors. If you moved, thought, felt, just as they did; and just as they, you did what was prescribed for a given moment. If, year after year, duties and rituals became part of you, and you took a wife, brought up children, and could meet peacefully the darkening days of old age.

Think of those who were refused a blessed resemblance to their fellow men. Of those who tried hard to act correctly, so that they would be spoken of no worse than their kin, but who did not succeed in anything, for whom everything would go wrong because of some invisible flaw. And who at last for that undeserved affliction would receive the punishment of loneliness, and who did not even try then to hide their fate.

On a bench in a public park, with a paper bag from which the neck of a bottle protrudes, under the bridges of the big cities, on sidewalks where the homeless keep their bundles, in a slum street with neon, waiting in front of a bar for the hour of opening, they, a nation of the excluded, whose day begins and ends with the awareness of failure. Think, how great is your luck. You did not even have to notice such as they, even though there were many nearby. Praise mediocrity and rejoice that you did not have to associate yourself with rebels. For, after all, they also were bearers of disagreement with the laws of life, and exaggerated hope, just like those who were marked in advance to fail.

CZESLAW MILOSZ

DENIAL

There's always someone worse off
and so you are speechless, paralyzed
as in those months on the orthopedic ward
when nothing moved from the waist down
but the pain.
And afterward the slow recovery,

bargaining inch by inch with the unknown
(if only to sit, to stand, to walk),
the patience learned inside a hurt
so severe that I discovered
there can be pain
more protracted than childbirth.

How can you speak for your own pain
remembering the gurney rides to the rehab gym
and the door open
on children from the Burn Unit
dipped into the centrifuge,
their skin flaked off in that swirling water.

The years accumulate. It's no longer the pain,
but not to have spoken of it,
the learned pattern of denial, that is never over.

KINERETH GENSLER

DON'T TELL A SOUL

Don't tell a soul.
Forget all you've seen—
A bird, an old woman, a jail,
Everything . . .

Or else when you open your mouth
At break of day
You'll tremble
Like the needles on a pine tree.

You'll remember the wasp at the cottage,
Your first pencil case,
Or the berries in the woods,
The ones you never picked.

OSIP MANDELSTAM

THE OTHER VOICES

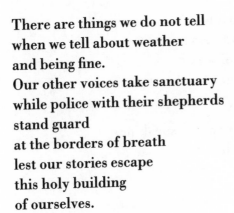

There are things we do not tell
when we tell about weather
and being fine.
Our other voices take sanctuary
while police with their shepherds
stand guard
at the borders of breath
lest our stories escape
this holy building
of ourselves.

How did we come to be
so unlike the chickens
clucking their hearts out
openly in the rain,
the horses just being horses
on the hillside,
and coyotes howling
their real life at the moon?

We don't tell our inner truth
and no one believes it anyway.
No wonder I am lying
in the sagging bed,
this body with the bad ankle
and fifteen scars showing,
and in the heart, my god,
the horrors of living.
And in my veins, dear mother,

the beauties of my joyous life,
the ribs and skull and being,
the eyes with real smiles
despite the sockets they live in
that know where they are going.

Outside, the other voices are speaking.
Pine needles sing with rain
and a night crawler,
with its five hearts
beats it
across the road.

In silence
the other voices speak
and they are mine
and they are not mine
and I hear them
and I don't,
and even police can't stop earth telling.

LINDA HOGAN

IN MY COUNTRY

In my country they jail you
for what they think you think.
My uncle once said to me:
they'll implant a microchip
in our minds
to flash our thoughts and dreams
onto a screen at John Vorster Square.
I was scared:
by day I guard my tongue
by night my dreams.

PITIKA NTULI

THE DEMOCRATIC JUDGE

In Los Angeles, before the judge who examines
  people
Trying to become citizens of the United States
Came an Italian restaurant keeper. After grave
  preparations
Hindered, though, by his ignorance of the new
  language
In the test he replied to the question:
What is the 8th Amendment? falteringly:
1492. Since the law demands that applicants know
  the language
He was refused. Returning
After three months spent on further studies
Yet hindered still by ignorance of the new language
He was confronted this time with the question:
  Who was
The victorious general in the Civil War? His
  answer was:
1492. (Given amiably, in a loud voice). Sent
  away again
And returning a third time, he answered
A third question: For how long a term are our
  Presidents elected?
Once more with: 1492. Now
The judge, who liked the man, realised that he
  could not
Learn the new language, asked him

How he earned his living and was told: by hard work.
  And so
At his fourth appearance the judge gave him
  the question:
When
Was America discovered? And on the strength of his
  correctly answering
1492, he was granted his citizenship.

BERTOLT BRECHT

THE BODY POLITIC

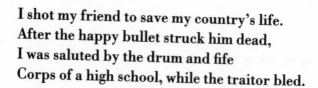

I shot my friend to save my country's life.
After the happy bullet struck him dead,
I was saluted by the drum and fife
Corps of a high school, while the traitor bled.

I understood the duty they assigned
And shot my friend to save my sanity;
Keeping disorder from the state of mind
Was mental hygiene, as it seemed to me.

I never thought until I pulled the trigger
But that I did the difficult and good;
I thought republics stood for something bigger,
For the mind of man, as Plato said they stood.

Correct in politics, I felt depressed.
How could this be? Guilty, I walked to where
My orders issued from, or so I guessed.
Nothing was there, nothing, nothing but air.

Talkative Socrates committed treason
Against instinct and natural emotion
By drinking hemlock on behalf of reason.
Too late I learn: A nation's just a notion.

DONALD HALL

SMALL HEART

—for Jan Józef Szczepański

The bullet that I shot
at the time of the great war
made a circle around the globe
and struck me in the back

at the least suitable moment
when I was already sure
I had forgotten everything
his-my faults

after all just like others
I wanted to erase from memory
the faces of hatred

history consoled me
that I had fought with naked force
and the Book said
—it is he who is Cain

so many years patiently
so many years in vain
with water of compassion I washed away
soot blood insults
so nobility
the beauty of existence
and perhaps even goodness
could have a home in me

after all just like everyone
I longed to return
to the bay of childhood
to the land of innocence

the bullet I shot
from a small calibre weapon
circled the globe
against the laws of gravitation
and struck me in the back
as if it wanted to say
—that nothing will be forgiven
to anyone

so now I sit alone
on the cut stump of a tree
exactly in the centre
of the forgotten battle

and I
gray spider
weave bitter meditations

about too great a memory
about too small a heart

ZBIGNIEW HERBERT

BILINGUAL SESTINA

Some things I have to say aren't getting said
in this snowy, blonde, blue-eyed, gum chewing English,
dawn's early light sifting through the *persianas* closed
the night before by dark-skinned girls whose words
evoke *cama, aposento, sueños* in *nombres*
from that first word I can't translate from Spanish.

Gladys, Rosario, Altagracia—the sounds of Spanish
wash over me like warm island waters as I say
your soothing names: a child again learning the
    nombres
of things you point to in the world before English
turned *sol, tierra, cielo, luna* to vocabulary words—
sun, earth, sky, moon—language closed

like the touch-sensitive *morivivir* whose leaves closed
when we kids poked them, astonished. Even Spanish
failed us then when we realized how frail a word
is when faced with the thing it names. How saying
its name won't always summon up in Spanish or
    English
the full blown genii from the bottled *nombre.*

Gladys, I summon you back with your given *nombre*
to open up again the house of slatted windows closed
since childhood, where *palabras* left behind for English
stand dusty and awkward in neglected Spanish.
Rosario, muse of *el patio*, sing in me and through me
    say
that world again, begin first with those first words

you put in my mouth as you pointed to the world—
not Adam, not God, but a country girl numbering
the stars, the blades of grass, warming the sun by
   saying
el sol as the dawn's light fell through the closed
persianas from the gardens where you sang in Spanish,
Esta son las mañanitas, and listening, in bed, no
   English

yet in my head to confuse me with translations, no
   English

doubling the world with synonyms, no dizzying array
   of words,
—the world was simple and intact in Spanish
awash with *colores, luz, sueños,* as if the *nombres*
were the outer skin of things, as if words were so close
to the world one left a mist of breath on things by
   saying

their names, an intimacy I now yearn for in English—
words so close to what I meant that I almost hear my
   Spanish
blood beating, beating inside what I say *en inglés.*

JULIA ALVAREZ

SMOKE AND DECEPTION

from Anton Chekhov's *The Privy Councillor*

When after supper Tatyana Ivanovna sat quietly down and took up her knitting, he kept his eyes fixed on her fingers and chatted away without ceasing.

"Make all the haste you can to live, my friends . . ." he said. "God forbid you should sacrifice the present for the future! There is youth, health, fire in the present; the future is smoke and deception! As soon as you are twenty, begin to live."

Tatyana Ivanovna dropped a knitting-needle.

RAYMOND CARVER

from CARTOGRAPHIES OF SILENCE

1.

A conversation begins
with a lie. And each

speaker of the so-called common language feels
the ice-floe split, the drift apart

as if powerless, as if up against
a force of nature

A poem can begin
with a lie. And be torn up.

A conversation has other laws
recharges itself with its own

false energy. Cannot be torn
up. Infiltrates our blood. Repeats itself.

Inscribes with its unreturning stylus
the isolation it denies.

2.

The classical music station
playing hour upon hour in the apartment

the picking up and picking up
and again picking up the telephone

The syllables uttering
the old script over and over

The loneliness of the liar
living in the formal network of the lie

twisting the dials to drown the terror
beneath the unsaid word

ADRIENNE RICH

WHEN MY LOVE SWEARS THAT
SHE IS MADE OF TRUTH

When my love swears that she is made of truth,
I do believe her, though I know she lies,
That she might think me some untutor'd youth,
Unlearned in the world's false subtleties.
Thus vainly thinking that she thinks me young,
Although she knows my days are past the best,
Simply I credit her false-speaking tongue:
On both sides thus is simple truth suppress'd.
But wherefore says she not she is unjust?
And wherefore say not I that I am old?
O, love's best habit is in seeming trust,
And age in love loves not to have years told:
  Therefore I lie with her and she with me,
  And in our faults by lies we flatter'd be.

WILLIAM SHAKESPEARE

from FRAGMENT 26

Often those I love best
          hurt me
most . . .

I know this is true.

SAPPHO

CRUSH

it was the eighties: i was wearing blue eye shadow,
carrying a pouchy headbanger purse with a rabbit's
foot dangling off one end, & listening to ac/dc. those
of you who remember those days are probably
groaning. i remember being offered a joint in phys ed
class, which i politely refused. caught between
wannabe bad girl & good chinese girl, i usually chose
the safe route. fitting into the times, the school, the
neighbourhood meant looking like a dopehead, but i
was too well-trained to act like one. meant ignoring
the boy by my locker, the one i had a crush on, when
he turned to the girls beside him & said something
about a chink. the same boy i had once played tag
with in elementary was now an expert in adolescent
cruelty & there was nothing i could do. i think he's
an accountant now. i hope he's gotten over the cruel
stage. i know i got over him that day.

RITA WONG

APPEAL

Daphnis dearest, wherefore weave me
Webs of lies lest truth should grieve me?
I could pardon much, believe me:
Dower me, Daphnis, or bereave me,
Kill me, kill me, love me, leave me—
Damn me, dear, but don't deceive me!

EDITH NESBIT

A RENEWAL

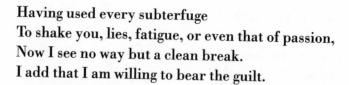

Having used every subterfuge
To shake you, lies, fatigue, or even that of passion,
Now I see no way but a clean break.
I add that I am willing to bear the guilt.

You nod assent. Autumn turns windy, huge,
A clear vase of dry leaves vibrating on and on.
We sit, watching. When I next speak
Love buries itself in me, up to the hilt.

JAMES MERRILL

HOW SHE RESOLVED TO ACT

"I shall be careful to say nothing at all
About myself or what I know of him
Or the vaguest thought I have—no matter how dim,
Tonight if it so happen that he call."

And not ten minutes later the doorbell rang
And into the hall he stepped as he always did
With a face and a bearing that quite poorly hid
His brain that burned and his heart that fairly sang
And his tongue that wanted to be rid of the truth.

As well as she could, for she was very loath
To signify how she felt, she kept very still,
But soon her heart cracked loud as a coffee mill
And her brain swung like a comet in the dark
And her tongue raced like a squirrel in the park.

MERRILL MOORE

WITH THE DOOR OPEN

Something I want to communicate to you,
I keep my door open between us.
I am unable to say it,
I am happy only
with the door open between us.

DAVID IGNATOW

A SECRET KEPT

A girl brought me into the house of love,
A girl as pure and perfect as Abigail,
And taking off her clothes, she revealed a body
So dazzling, it beggared comparison.
Her light shining in the darkness made everything
    tremble,
The hills began dancing like rams.
"O Lord," I thought, "our secrets will be
    discovered,"
But she reached back at once with her powerful
    hands
And covered us both with her long black hair,
And once again it was night.

JUDAH AL-HARIZI

HIDING OUR LOVE

Never believe I leave you
From any desire to go.
Never believe I live so far away
Except from necessity.
After a whole day of separation
Still your dark fragrance clings to my skin.
I carry your letter everywhere.
The sash of my dress wraps twice around my waist.
I wish it bound the two of us together.

Do you know that we both conceal our love
Because of prior sorrow, superstitious fear?
We are two citizens of a savage era
Schooled in disguises and in self-command,
Hiding our aromatic, vulnerable love.

CAROLYN KIZER
(based on a poem by the Emperor Wu-ti)

AND THE DAYS ARE NOT FULL ENOUGH

And the days are not full enough
And the nights are not full enough
And life slips by like a field mouse
        Not shaking the grass.

EZRA POUND

I AM ASKING YOU TO COME BACK HOME

I am asking you to come back home
before you lose your chance of seein' me alive.
You already missed your daddy.
You missed your Uncle Howard.
You missed Luciel. I kept them and I buried them.
You showed up for the funerals.
Funerals are the easy part.

You even missed that dog you left.
I dug him a hole and put him in it.
It was a Sunday morning but dead animals
don't wait no better than dead people.

My mama used to say she could feel herself
runnin' short of the breath of life. So can I.
And I am blessed tired of buryin' things I love.
Somebody else can do that job to me.
You'll be back here then, you come for funerals.

I'd rather you come back now and got my stories.
I've got whole lives of stories that belong to you.
I could fill you up with stories,
stories I ain't told nobody yet,
stories with your name, your blood in them.
Ain't nobody gonna hear them if you don't
and you ain't gonna hear them unless you get back
    home.

When I am dead, it will not matter
how hard you press your ear to the ground.

JO CARSON

HYPOCRISY

HYPOCRISY will serve as well
To propagate a church, as zeal;
As persecution and promotion
Do equally advance devotion;
So round white stones will serve, they say,
As well as eggs to make hens lay.

SAMUEL BUTLER

SOUS-ENTENDU

Don't think

that I don't know
that as you talk to me
the hand of your mind
is inconspicuously
taking off my stocking,
moving in resourceful blindness
up along my thigh.

Don't think
that I don't know
that you know
everything I say
is a garment.

ANNE STEVENSON

THE LIE

Go soul the body's guest
 upon a thankless errand,
Fear not to touch the best
 the truth shall be thy warrant:
Go since I needs must die,
 and give the world the lie.

Say to the Court it glows
 and shines like rotten wood,
Say to the Church it shows
 what's good, and doth no good;
If Church and Court reply,
 then give them both the lie.

Tell Potentates they live
 acting by others' action,
Not loved unless they give,
 not strong but by affection;
If Potentates reply
 give Potentates the lie.

Tell men of high condition
 that manage the estate,
Their purpose is ambition,
 their practice only hate,
And if they once reply
 then give them all the lie.

Tell them that brave it most,
    they beg for more by spending,
Who in their greatest cost
    seek nothing but commending.
And if they make reply,
    then give them all the lie.

Tell zeal it wants devotion
    tell love it is but lust
Tell time it metes but motion,
    tell flesh it is but dust.
And wish them not reply
    for thou must give the lie.

Tell age it daily wasteth,
    tell honour how it alters.
Tell beauty how she blasteth,
    tell favour how it falters;
And as they shall reply,
    give every one the lie.

Tell wit how much it wrangles
    in tickle points of niceness,
Tell wisdom she entangles
    herself in over wiseness.
And when they do reply
    straight give them both the lie.

Tell Physic of her boldness,
    tell skill it is prevention:
Tell charity of coldness,
    tell law it is contention,
And as they do reply
    so give them still the lie.

Tell fortune of her blindness,
    tell nature of decay,
Tell friendship of unkindness,
    tell justice of delay.
And if they will reply,
    then give them all the lie.

Tell Arts they have no soundness,
    but vary by esteeming,
Tell schools they want profoundness
    and stand too much on seeming.
If Arts and schools reply,
    give arts and schools the lie.

Tell faith it's fled the City,
    tell how the country erreth,
Tell manhood shakes off pity,
    tell virtue least preferreth;
And if they do reply
    spare not to give the lie.

So when thou hast as I
   commanded thee, done blabbing,
although to give the lie,
   deserves no less than stabbing.
Stab at thee he that will,
   no stab thy soul can kill.

SIR WALTER RALEGH

COME ALL YOU FAIR AND TENDER LADIES

Come all you fair and tender ladies,
Be careful how you court young men,
They're like a star of a summer's morning,
They'll first appear and then they're gone.

They'll tell to you some loving story,
They'll declare to you their love is true;
Straightway they'll go and court some other,
And that's the love they have for you.

I wish I was some little sparrow,
That I had wings, could fly so high;
I'd fly away to my false true lover,
And when he's talkin' I'd be by.

But I am not a little sparrow,
And neither have I wings to fly;
I'll sit down here in grief and sorrow
To weep and pass my troubles by.

If I'd a-known before I courted,
I never would have courted none;
I'd have locked my heart in a box of golden,
And pinned it up with a silver pin.

ANONYMOUS

SONG

Tell me no more I am deceived;
    While Silvia seems so kind,
And takes such care to be believed,
    The cheat I fear to find.
To flatter me, should falsehood lie
    Concealed in her soft youth,
A thousand times I'd rather die
    Than see the unhappy truth.

My love all malice shall outbrave,
    Let fops in libels rail;
If she the appearances will save,
    No scandal can prevail.
She makes me think I have her heart,
    How much for that is due?
Though she but act the tender part,
    The joy she gives is true.

SIR GEORGE ETHEREGE

THE FOOL'S SONG

I tried to put a bird in a cage.
     Oh fool that I am!
  For the bird was Truth.
Sing merrily, Truth: I tried to put
     Truth in a cage!

And when I had the bird in the cage,
     O fool that I am!
  Why, it broke my pretty cage.
Sing merrily, Truth: I tried to put
     Truth in a cage!

And when the bird was flown from the cage,
     O fool that I am!
  Why, I had not bird nor cage.
Sing merrily, Truth: I tried to put
     Truth in a cage!
  Heigh-ho! Truth in a cage.

WILLIAM CARLOS WILLIAMS

TO A FRIEND WHOSE WORK HAS COME TO NOTHING

Now all the truth is out,
Be secret and take defeat
From any brazen throat,
For how can you compete,
Being honor bred, with one
Who, were it proved he lies
Were neither shamed in his own
Nor in his neighbors' eyes?
Bred to a harder thing
Than Triumph, turn away
And like a laughing string
Whereon mad fingers play
Amid a place of stone,
Be secret and exult,
Because of all things known
That is most difficult.

WILLIAM BUTLER YEATS

THE CLAY JUG

Inside this clay jug there are canyons and pine
    mountains
and the maker of canyons and pine mountains!
All seven oceans are inside, and hundreds of millions
    of stars.
The acid that tests gold is there, and the one who
    judges jewels.
And the music from the strings that no one touches,
    and the source of all water.

If you want the truth, I will tell you the truth:
Friend, listen: the God I love is inside.

KABIR

A BOX CALLED THE IMAGINATION

Knock on a wall with your knuckle—
from the piece of oak
a cuckoo
will jump out

it calls forth trees
one and another
until a forest
is standing

whistle lightly—
a river will flow
a powerful thread
binding mountains with valleys

make a sound—
here is the city
with one tower
a jagged wall
and yellow houses
like dice

now
close your eyes
snow will fall
will extinguish
the green flickers of trees
the red tower

under the snow
it is night
with a clock shining at the top
the owl of the landscape

ZBIGNIEW HERBERT

THE GIRL WHO BECAME MY GRANDMOTHER

Every night after the household was asleep, the girl who became my grandmother rode her stove through the forests of Lithuania.

She would return by dawn, her black hair gleaming with droplets of dew and her burlap sack filled with fog-webbed mushrooms and roots.

"It's true," my grandfather said. "At first I followed, but I could never keep up." He would hear the clanging and rusty squeakings fade into the trees and, with a sigh, he would go home.

He accepted the situation until the night she left in the kitchen, as if she were riding in a coach pulled by black horses of wind.

Grandfather followed in the rest of the house, standing in the doorway to the now-departed room, bellowing threats as if urging the house forward at greater speed.

He caught her outside Vilna, when she stopped to get her bearings, and the house slammed into the stalled kitchen, grandfather tumbling through the doorway and hitting his head on the leg of a table.

"And where do you think you're going this time, Lady?" he groaned from the floor, rubbing his right ear.

The girl smiled down at him and, kneeling by his side, stroked his hair, but didn't say anything.

That was the last time the girl who became my grandmother went on a nocturnal outing. Soon after, they left for America.

In Brooklyn, she rode from one day to the next in the house he had built around her, watching the changing scene beyond the kitchen window.

It was then she became my grandmother, white-haired and smiling, never saying much of anything, even when the old man shouted from the other rooms. Not that he ever needed anything. He just wanted to be sure she was still there.

MORTON MARCUS

THE WAY THROUGH THE WOODS

They shut the road through the woods
Seventy years ago.
Weather and rain have undone it again,
And now you would never know
There was once a road through the woods

Before they planted the trees.
It is underneath the coppice and heath
And the thin anemones.
Only the keeper sees
That, where the ring-dove broods,
And the badgers roll at ease,
There was once a road through the woods.

Yet, if you enter the woods
Of a summer evening late,
When the night-air cools on the trout-ringed pools
Where the otter whistles his mate,
(They fear not men in the woods,
Because they see so few.)
You will hear the beat of a horse's feet,
And the swish of a skirt in the dew,
Steadily cantering through
The misty solitudes,
As though they perfectly knew
The old lost road through the woods . . .
But there is no road through the woods.

RUDYARD KIPLING

NOT FOREVER ON EARTH

Can it be true we live on earth?
Not forever on earth: only a brief moment here.
Even jade shatters.
Even gold breaks.
Even the plumage of the quetzal tears apart.
Not forever on earth: only a brief moment here.

KING NEZAHUALCOYOTL

NO HELP FOR THAT

there is a place in the heart that
will never be filled

a space

and even during the
best moments
and
the greatest
times

we will know it

we will know it

we will know it
more than
ever

there is a place in the heart that
will never be filled

and we will wait
and wait

in that
space

CHARLES BUKOWSKI

BIOGRAPHICAL NOTES

Quotes within the biographies are from interviews, letters, or readily available sources, such as the World Wide Web.

Julia Alvarez (b. 1950) was ten years old when her family returned to the United States, fleeing the Dominican Republic because of her father's participation in an unsuccessful attempt to overthrow the Trujillo dictatorship. As a teen in New York City, she decided she wanted to be a writer, and the uprooting she experienced as a girl became the theme of her first two novels: *How the Garcia Girls Lost Their Accents* and *In the Time of the Butterflies.* About writing Alvarez says, "I write to find out what I'm thinking. I write to find out who I am. I write to understand things."

Suggested Reading:
   Homecoming (poems; NAL Dutton)
   The Other Side/El Otro Lado (poems; NAL Dutton)
   Something to Declare (a book of essays about writing and her life; Algonquin Books)

Yehuda Amichai (b. 1924), Israel's most popular poet, was born in Germany; he and his family immigrated to Israel in 1936. He's the author of eleven books of poetry in Hebrew, two novels, a book of short stories, essays, and reviews. His writing has been translated into thirty-three languages. Amichai began writing when he was in the army: "I never wrote during battles, but sometimes between battles I wrote what were almost small testaments, small legacies, last wills, objects of feeling I could keep and carry with me." It wasn't until later, at the age of twenty-five, when, as

Amichai observes, "the writing I was reading didn't represent my needs, what I saw and what I felt," that he began to write poetry.

"Irony is integral to my poetry," Amichai says (as is evident in his poem included in this collection). "Irony is, for me, a kind of cleaning material. . . . Irony is a way of focusing, unfocusing, and focusing again—always trying to see another side . . . that's the way I live—focusing, refocusing, and juxtaposing different shifting and changing perspectives."

Suggested Reading:

A Great Tranquility: Questions and Answers (poems; Sheep Meadow Press)

Poems of Jerusalem and Love Poems (Sheep Meadow Press)

The Selected Poetry of Yehuda Amichai: Newly Revised and Expanded Edition (University of California Press)

Margaret Atwood (b. 1939) was born in Ontario, and because her father was a forest entomologist, she spent a great deal of her childhood living in a cabin in the Canadian wilderness. By the age of six, she was writing "poems, morality plays, comic books, and an unfinished novel about an ant." Just ten years later, she decided she wanted to be a writer. As Atwood explains, she wanted "to live a double life; to go places I haven't been; to examine life on earth; to come to know people in ways and at depths, that are otherwise impossible; to be surprised . . . to give back something of what [I have] received."

Atwood is best known for her fiction, which includes *The Edible Woman*, *Surfacing*, and *Alias Grace*. Made into a feature film, her 1985 novel, *The Handmaid's Tale*, is a rather horrifying and convincing book about a future time when women are no longer allowed to read and are valued only for their fertility. It explores the complex issues of freedom, power, control, what is true, and what is a lie.

Atwood is also a poet and the author of several children's books as well as television and radio scripts.

Suggested Reading:
   Morning in the Burned House (poems; Houghton Mifflin)
   The Handmaid's Tale (a novel; Doubleday)
   Wilderness Tips (a novel; Bantam)

William Blake (1757–1827) was a child of spiritual inclinations who, at ten, tried to convince his father that he'd seen angels up in a tree. Throughout his life Blake felt connected with the spirits, angels, and devils that became the subjects of his poetry. He published his first poems when he was in his mid-twenties, served as an engraver for a London bookseller, and later set up his own print shop. The year 1789 marked the beginning of a time of great creativity for Blake, and his major works were written and published during a relatively short period.

Suggested Reading:
   Blake: Complete Writings (edited by Geoffrey Keynes; Oxford University Press)
   Songs of Innocence and Experience (poems; Orion Press)

Playwright **Bertolt Brecht** (1898–1956) was born and raised in Germany. He was greatly influenced by the two world wars and the impact of Communism and Nazism on society. His work focused on the subject of alienation; he valued not the individual and private life but social truth, and he attempted to communicate this to the audience by encouraging them to think rather than to identify with characters. Brecht developed his drama as a forum for leftist causes. During the height of his popularity, in the forties and fifties, he was the darling of the literati, considered avant-garde because his work was new and gritty. Experimental drama still looks to him. Though best known for his plays, Brecht was also a poet.

Suggested Reading:

Selected Poems of Bertholt Brecht (Methuen/Routledge)

The Threepenny Opera; The Measure Taken; Galileo; Mother Courage and Her Children (plays; German Library, vol. 75)

Charles Bukowski (1920–1994) published his first story when he was twenty-four. During his life he produced more than sixty volumes of poetry and prose. His father's abuse made his childhood a very difficult one. When Bukowski mentions his father in his work, he usually includes descriptions of his father's anger and stories of being beaten with a strap. He wrote, "When they beat you long enough and hard enough, you have the tendency to say what you really mean; in other words, they take all the pretenses out of you." As an adolescent he suffered from horrible acne and said that the only ones who wanted to be his friends were the poor, the lost, and the idiots. With his writing he became a spokesman for them. For many years Bukowski worked at a Los Angeles post office, in addition to having been a dishwasher, truckdriver, guard, gas station attendant, Red Cross orderly, and elevator operator. Bukowski possessed a keen ear for the music of everyday speech and an ability to find meaning and beauty in even the dreadful moments of life.

Suggested Reading:

Betting on the Muse: Poems & Stories (Black Sparrow Press)

Ham on Rye (a memoir; Black Sparrow Press)

Post Office: A Novel (Black Sparrow Press)

Of Puerto Rico's most famous poet **Julia de Burgos** (1914–1953), the great Chilean poet Pablo Neruda said that her calling was to be a great poet of the Americas. De Burgos lived a short and passionate life committed to poetry and the independence of her country. Even before a volume of her poems was published, she was considered a poet of great stature. At twenty-two she was elected secretary general of the nonpartisan Women's United Front for a Constitutional Convention. Her political work also included membership in a committee to free several countrymen imprisoned for their efforts on behalf of Puerto Rico's independence. During her lifetime only two collections of her poetry were published. De Burgos's poetry broke new ground by blending a romantic temperament with astute political awareness. She died a pauper at the age of thirty-nine in New York City.

Suggested Reading:

Song of the Simple Truth: The Complete Poems of Julia de Burgos (a bilingual edition translated by Jack Agüeros; Curbstone Press)

Diane Burns (b. 1950), most recently from Wisconsin, is the author of the book of poems *Riding the One-Eyed Ford*, which was nominated for the William Carlos Williams Award. She attended the Institute of American Indian Art in New Mexico, where she was awarded the Congressional Medal of Merit for academic and artistic excellence. She later attended Barnard College.

Samuel Butler (1612–1680) was an English poet and satirist. His skill in both roles is evident in his poem included in this collection. He's best known for his work *Hudibras*, a satire against Puritanism. His sage advice includes, "Life is the art of drawing sufficient conclusions from insufficient premises."

Jo Carson (b. 1946) is a writer and performer from Johnson City, Tennessee. She has published plays, short stories, books for children, essays, poems, and other work. Carson has won a series of national awards for plays, and her most recent play, *Whispering to Horses*, won an AT&T Onstage: New Plays for the '90s Award. She is currently the recipient of a Theater Communications Group/NEA residency award to work with seven stages in Atlanta, Georgia.

Able to live well on little money, Carson has made her living at writing and performing for more than fifteen years. She drives a pickup truck because it is large and she isn't.

Suggested Reading:
The Last of the Waltz Around Texas and Other Stories (Gnomon Press)
Stories I Ain't Told Nobody Yet (Orchard Books)

Known best for his short stories, **Raymond Carver** (1938–1989) was also an accomplished poet. Toward the end of his life, when he was sick with cancer, he wrote his last book of poems, *A New Path to the Waterfall*, which was published after his death. During the time of his illness, the poet Tess Gallagher, Carver's wife, was reading the short stories of Chekhov, which she would retell to Carver. Later he'd read the story himself. Both Carver and Gallagher turned to Chekhov frequently throughout the painful time of his illness. And Carver began marking passages of the stories and retyping them, putting the excerpts into the shape of poems. Carver's final book is interspersed with these poems that he found within Chekhov's stories.

Suggested Reading:
A New Path to the Waterfall (poems; The Atlantic Monthly Press)
Where I'm Calling From, New and Selected Stories (Vintage Contemporaries)

Anton Chekhov (1860–1904), a Russian doctor and writer of plays and short stories, said, "A writer is not a confectioner, a cosmetic dealer, or an entertainer. He is a man who has signed a contract with his conscience and his sense of duty." Chekhov was born in 1860, and while he was still a student he helped to support his family by selling humorous stories to magazines. His first collection of short stories was published when he was twenty-four, the year he graduated from college. He is considered a master of short fiction.

In the last few years of his life, Chekhov wrote four plays, which established him as a great playwright, including *The Seagull* and *The Cherry Orchard*. He died in 1904 of tuberculosis.

Suggested Reading:
The Essential Tales of Chekhov (edited by Richard Ford; The Ecco Press)

Cheryl Clarke (b. 1947), an African-American lesbian feminist poet, is the author of four books of poetry, including *Narratives: Poems in the Tradition of Black Women* and *Experimental Love*, which was a Lambda Literary Award finalist. Of the role of truth and lies in her writing Clarke notes, "Truth is somebody else's lies and lies are somebody else's truths. Both exist in my poetry."

Lucille Clifton (b. 1936) has said, "[T]he proper subject matter for poetry is life . . . I write about being human. If you have ever been human, I invite you to that place we share." Her work reminds us of our own humanness in language that resounds with the emotion and details of life. Langston Hughes was the first to publish her work, which appeared in the anthology *Poetry of the Negro*. Clifton went to Howard University; she was the first person in her family to finish high school and enter college. It was at the university that she said, "I'm going to write poems. I can do what I want to do! I'm from Dahomey women!" Her first book of poems, *Good Times*, was published when she was thirty-nine, and twice she's been nominated for the Pulitzer Prize. Clifton is also the author of more than sixteen children's books; she's well known for her Everett Anderson series. Clifton is the mother of six children and currently lives in Maryland.

Suggested Reading:
Good Woman: Poems and a Memoir, 1969–1980 (BOA Editions)

The Book of Light (poems; BOA Editions)
The Terrible Stories (poems; BOA Editions)

The author of **"Come All You Fair and Tender Ladies"** is unknown. There are many versions of this song in which a young woman compares men to the stars of a summer morning that first appear and then they're gone. She wishes she were a sparrow or, in some versions, a swallow, so she could fly to a particular young man and, without his knowing, listen to what he says. There's also a connection between this song and another traditional song in which a convict in a state prison wishes he had the wings of a sparrow to fly to the arms of his mother and lie down and die. "Come All You Fair and Tender Ladies" is also called "Little Sparrow." Under various titles and with considerable variation in text, it's known as a traditional song in Virginia, Kentucky, Tennessee, Georgia, North Carolina, Indiana, and other states.

Stephen Crane (1871–1900) grew up in a rigid religious environment; both his parents were ministers. He didn't like religion or school; at Syracuse University he was noted for playing baseball. Crane lived the life of a penniless artist and became well known as a poet, journalist, and social critic. He earned international recognition at twenty-four for his book *The Red Badge of Courage*. As a journalist he covered the Greco-Turkish War and later the Spanish-American War. Toward the end of his life, even though he suffered from tuberculosis, he wrote furiously, attempting to cover his debts. He died in Germany at twenty-nine.

Suggested Reading:
   The Red Badge of Courage (a novel; Random House)
   Great Short Works of Stephen Crane: Red Badge of Courage, Monster, Maggie, Open Boat, Blue Hotel, Bride Comes to Yellow Sky, and Other Works (HarperCollins)

The **Crow people** migrated to the Great Plains (Montana-Wyoming area) in the 1700s. The American name Crow comes from the tribe's own name for themselves, Apsaalooke, "Children of the Long-Beaked Bird" or "Raven." The Crow were known for their openness to other peoples (except war enemies), generosity, and commitment to tribe members, particularly children, and for their many songs and dances that celebrated life and the Great Spirit.

The Crow had good reason to sing about deception as they did in "Song of the Bald Eagle." Their long history of cooperation with the settlers was repaid with broken treaties and unscrupulous land negotiations. The Crow people were forced onto reservations where a vigorous attempt was made to "de-Crow" their cultural traditions, and their wealth of songs and dances diminished and nearly disappeared.

Today many of the Crow raise horses and cattle on a two-million-acre reservation near the Bighorn Mountains in Montana, site of their ancestral homelands. They also husband a herd of wild buffalo. Every August the Crow Fair celebrates "Buffalo Days," where the rich traditions of the Crow people are renewed in dance contests, rodeo competitions, drumming, horse races, and giveaways.

Suggested Reading:

Brave Wolf and the Thunderbird (picture-book retelling of a Crow Indian story by Joe Medicine Crow; Tales of the People Series, Abbeville Press)

The Crow (young-adult book by Frederick E. Hoxie; Indians of North America Series, Chelsea House)

The Crow People (by Dale K. McGinnis and Floyd W. Sharrock; Indian Tribal Series in Phoenix)

Cortney Davis (b. 1945) is the author of two poetry collections and the coeditor of the anthology *Between the Heartbeats: Poetry and Prose by Nurses*. The recipient of an NEA poetry fellowship and two Connecticut Commission on the Arts grants, she has written poems that have recently appeared in *Poetry*, *Kalliope*, *Prairie Schooner*, and the *Massachusetts Review*. In addition to being a poet, Davis is a nurse practitioner.

A nonfiction book about her work in women's health, *All Desired Women*, is forthcoming from Random House.

Suggested Reading:
The Body Flute (poems; Adastra Press)
Details of Flesh (poems; CALYX Books)

Emily Dickinson (1830–1886) is considered the mother of American poetry, although she published only ten poems during her lifetime. She lived a solitary life, rarely leaving home. After her death 1,700 poems on scraps of paper, some of which she had bound into booklets, were discovered, and after heavy editing, some of them were published. It wasn't until 1955 that her poetry appeared in print as she had written it, frequently using dashes in place of more customary punctuation.

Suggested Reading:
The Complete Poems of Emily Dickinson (edited by Thomas H. Johnson; Little, Brown)
The Life of Emily Dickinson (by Richard B. Sewall; Harvard University Press)

The English dramatist **Sir George Etherege** (c. 1635–1691) was an ambassador for Charles II and, later, a representative for James II. The period during which Etherege lived, the Restoration, was marked by an increase in colonization, advances in trading, opposition to Roman Catholicism, and a revival of drama and poetry. Known as "Easy Etherege" by his friends, he was a conceited man preoccupied with his appearance.

Kinereth Gensler (b. 1922) grew up in Chicago and Jerusalem. As an undergraduate she attended the University of Chicago and then went to Columbia for graduate school. She lives in Cambridge, Massachusetts, where she has taught Radcliffe seminars for twenty years. Gensler is the author of three volumes of poetry from Alice James Books, including *Journey Fruit*, and she is the coeditor of the teaching anthology *The Poetry Connection*, a text for teaching poetry writing to children.

Gogisgi/Carroll Arnett (1927–1997), considered one of the most respected Native American poets of his generation, was born in Oklahoma City. Of his work the writer Joseph Bruchac said, "[T]he themes of clarity and honesty were always at the heart of all his writing. His poems consistently explore the truths of contemporary Native American life in ways that are sometimes painful, but always memorable and direct." Gogisgi, which means "Smoke" in Cherokee, was a former marine and a well-loved professor of literature at Michigan State University.

Suggested Reading:
  Spells (Bloody Twin Press)

Donald Hall (b. 1928) began writing poetry when he was twelve. In an interview in *The Atlantic Monthly*, Hall said, "[W]hen I was fourteen I got serious. I began to work a couple of hours every day on my poems. And when I got finished working on a poem, I would go back to the beginning and start writing it over again, revising. Nobody told me to do this; I don't know why I did. When I was fourteen I really wanted to do in my life what I in fact have more or less ended up doing."

After attending Phillips Exeter and Harvard University, he began teaching at the University of Michigan, where he taught for many years. It was there that he met the poet Jane Kenyon in 1969. They married and later made their home at Eagle Pond, his family's house, where Hall had written his first poems. Hall and Kenyon devoted themselves to writing and their life at Eagle Pond until her diagnosis of cancer. She died at the age of forty-seven in 1995.

Hall is the author of more than ten books of poetry, four plays, books for children, collected essays and short stories, textbooks, and more. He has received many awards, including a Caldecott Medal, the *Los Angeles Times* Book Prize in Poetry, the Lenore Marshall Award, and the Ruth Lilly Poetry Prize from the American Council for the Arts.

Suggested Reading:
The Old Life: Old and New Poems (Houghton Mifflin)
Without: Poems (Houghton Mifflin)
Life Work (a book about the meaning of work and its role in our lives; Beacon Press)

Judah al-Harizi (c. 1165–1225) was a Jew born in Muslim Spain during a period when Islamic culture flowered, in part because the Muslims were quite open to having Jews participate in society, whereas Christians were not. He lived much of his life in the Muslim East, where he sang the praises of powerful people in Egypt and Syria. A troubadour poet, al-Harizi began his career as a translator of Hebrew. He was known for his translation of Maimonides' *Guide to the Perplexed* into a language that was accessible to the average person. Al-Harizi was a master of the Hebrew *maqama*, a narrative written in rhymed prose interspersed with metrical poems.

In addition to being a poet, **Joy Harjo** (b. 1951), who was born in Tulsa, Oklahoma, is a musician who performs her poetry and plays saxophone in her band Poetic Justice, which won a 1998 Outstanding Musical Achievement Award. She has received such honors as the American Indian Distinguished Achievement in the Arts Award, the Josephine Miles Poetry Award, and the William Carlos Williams Award, among others. Having spent much of her life in the Southwest, and often considered a New Mexican writer, Harjo currently resides in Hawaii, drawn there by the Pacific Ocean.

She says about writing, "What I am moved by is the

strange and simple ironies of life, how beauty links up with terror, or how beauty survives the terrible often as a witness."

Suggested Reading:
A Map to the Next World, Poems and Tales (W. W. Norton)
The Woman Who Fell from the Sky (poems; W. W. Norton)
The Spiral of Memory: Interviews (Poets on Poetry)
Letter from the End of the Twentieth Century (CD; Silver Wave Records)

Zbigniew Herbert (1924–1998), a spiritual leader of the anti-Communist movement in Poland, knew intimately about living under occupation. He was a teenager when the Nazis ravaged his country, and then Poland was taken over by another oppressor—Stalin. As a young man beginning to write poetry, Herbert was confronted with the awareness that if he wrote honestly, not only might his work not survive, but he might not as well. Much of his work deals with what it means to live in a country where others define and enforce what is acceptable to write and what is not. Rather than write under the government's official guidelines, he worked at many jobs that paid poorly. Herbert developed an underground reputation, and his work appeared, through translation, in western Europe and the United States. It wasn't until 1956, during a political thaw, that his first book was published in Poland. His work is associated with the renaissance of Polish poetry during the mid-fifties.

Herbert traveled extensively after the 1950s, writing, in addition to poetry, essays and stage and radio plays.

Suggested Reading:
Elegy for the Departure (poems; The Ecco Press)

Robert Herrick (1591–1674) was a leading Cavalier poet of seventeenth-century England. His father committed suicide shortly after Herrick's birth, and he was raised by a wealthy uncle, a goldsmith who apprenticed Herrick to the trade. Herrick showed more interest in poetry, however, so his uncle sent him to Cambridge University. In 1623 he became a priest in the Church of England. His loyalty to Charles I uprooted him from his position as vicar when the Commonwealth government took over.

Herrick's poetry ranges from odes and folk songs to epigrams and love lyrics. His poetry shows the influence of court musicians and his classical and theological training. *Hesperides*, a collection of 1,400 poems, is his one published book.

Jonell Hill (b. 1957) was raised in the Eastern Sierra of California. She now lives with her four children in the Santa Cruz Mountains. Her poetry has been published in various journals and literary magazines.

"I grew up believing that a lie was something one had to speak aloud," Hill says. "It was years before I came to realize that silence could also be a form of lying. Writing was, for me, as a young woman, the only way I felt comfortable speaking, and I know it now to be a sure and certain way to find what is truest in a thing."

Linda Hogan (b. 1947) has played a significant role in the development of contemporary Native American poetry and is dedicated to concerns for the environment, including antinuclear issues. Her love of story began with the gifts of Native American legends and the art of storytelling from her father and grandparents. Hogan first published her poetry when she was in her mid-twenties.

The sixteen-year-old Native American narrator of Hogan's novel *Power* says, in talking about her elders, "They remember what they were born knowing. Nothing replaced it or erased it like it has done with me. Me, I am a dissolved person, like salt in water."

Suggested Reading:
    Savings (poems; Coffee House Press)
    Power (novel; W. W. Norton)
    Solar Storms (a novel; Simon & Schuster)

David Ignatow (1914–1997) was born to immigrant parents in Brooklyn and lived most of his life in New York City. His early jobs included research writer, office manager, auto messenger, hospital admitting clerk, and paper salesman. Ignatow's first book of poems was published when he was in his mid-thirties. He established himself as a writer in the years following and worked on a series of editorships, including the William Carlos Williams memorial chapbook in 1963. His many awards include two Guggenheim Fellowships and the Bollingen Prize. In 1955 Ignatow's son developed a serious mental illness from which he did not recover. Ignatow described his writing after 1955 as the record of his son's illness and of his own return to faith years later.

Suggested Reading:
   Living Is What I Wanted: Last Poems (BOA Editions)
   New and Collected Poems (University Press of New England)

Juan Ramón Jiménez (1888–1958) spent his early years in Maguer, Spain, which would later become an affectionate subject of his writing. Although Jiménez began studying law and painting at the University of Seville, he gave up his studies to devote his time to his true love, poetry. He was invited to Madrid by other well-known poets who had seen his work, and he became involved in Modernist literary circles. His poems are impressionistic and lyrical, mysterious and metaphorical. He was deeply affected by the death of his father in 1900, and many of his poems show a preoccupation with death. Jiménez was a critic and editor for various literary journals, while producing several volumes of poetry. His experimentation with poetic form gained him worldwide attention, and he was awarded the Nobel Prize for Literature in 1956. That same year, his wife died, and, deeply saddened by this loss, Jiménez died two years later in Puerto Rico.

Suggested Reading:
Light and Shadows: Selected Poems and Prose (translated by James Wright et al.; White Pine Press)
Lorca and Jiménez: Selected Poems (edited by Robert Bly; Beacon Press)

Rodney Jones (b. 1950) was born in Alabama and educated at the universities of Alabama and North Carolina. In his poetry, Jones embraces his southern roots, and his topics range from football to verse, from animals to feminism—often poking fun at himself. He has won the National Book Critics Circle Award and the Jean Stein Award of the American Academy of Arts and Letters. He is now a professor of English at the University of Southern Illinois at Carbondale.

Suggested Reading:
Apocalyptic Narrative and Other Poems (Houghton Mifflin)
Things That Happen Once (Houghton Mifflin)

Kabir (1398–1518) was born in India and is said to have lived for 120 years. Kabir, a weaver by profession, is often considered one of the greatest poets of the world. He criticized all sects and approached Indian philosophy in a new way. Some people consider Kabir a guru (a spiritual teacher) and say that his work can help people with their lives both spiritually and socially. His poems are simple and straightforward, often only two lines long, and have universal appeal.

Suggested Reading:
The Kabir Book (translated by Robert Bly; The Seventies Press, Beacon)
The Bijak of Kabir (edited and translated by Linda Hess; Farrar, Straus & Giroux)

Jackie Kay (b. 1961) was born and raised in Scotland. She is the author of three poetry collections for adults and three for children. Kay's work has garnered her a number of awards, including two Scottish Arts Council Book Awards and a Somerset Maugham Award. Her novel *Trumpet*, published in 1998, won the *Guardian* Fiction Prize. She says, "I have always enjoyed making things up and taking liberties with the truth since I was a child." In her writing she likes "crossing the border country between the imaginary world and the real world." She lives in Manchester, England, with her son.

Suggested Reading:

Other Lovers (poems; Bloodaxe)

Trumpet (a novel; Picador)

The Frog Who Dreamed She Was an Opera Singer (poems for children; Bloomsbury)

Rudyard Kipling (1865–1936) was born in Bombay to upper-class military parents who abandoned him in 1875, and he was brought back to England to live with a foster family. Before he was even twenty-five, he had gained recognition for his stories of Anglo-Indian life. Kipling is best known for his children's books *Just So Stories* and *The Jungle Book*. Although he became the first English writer to receive the Nobel Prize in 1907, his popularity was on the decline because of his racist views and reactionary politics. Yet Kipling was also a warm man and a loving father whose life was filled with great sorrows, including the death of his only son in WWI. Following the illness of his six-year-old daughter, his sister said, "He was a sadder and a harder man." Kipling died in 1936.

Suggested Reading:

The Jungle Book (NTC Contemporary)

Just So Stories (Penguin USA)

Rudyard Kipling: A Life (by Harry Rickets; Carroll & Graf)

Carolyn Kizer (b. 1925) was born in Spokane, Washington. Between 1964 and 1966 she was the Specialist in Literature for the U.S. State Department in Pakistan, and in 1966 she was appointed the first director of literature programs for the National Endowment for the Arts. She resigned the post in 1970 when President Nixon fired the chairman of the NEA. Kizer is the author of seven books of poetry. Her many awards include the Pulitzer Prize, The Frost Medal and Masefield Prize of the Poetry Society of America, the Pushcart Prize, and others. Kizer is a former chancellor of the Academy of American Poets and lives in Sonoma, California, and Paris.

Kizer's poem *Hiding Our Love* is based on a poem by the Chinese emperor Wu-ti, who lived from 140 B.C.E. to 87 B.C.E. During his reign of the former Han dynasty, the emperor engaged in many foreign wars, which led to great territorial expansion. Wu-ti mobilized from fifty thousand to one hundred thousand soldiers, a far larger army than those of previous emperors. Through his efforts, which included the establishment of schools that taught only Confucian thought, Confucianism gained in popularity while Wu-ti was in power.

Suggested Reading:
Mermaids in the Basement: Poems for Women (Copper Canyon Press)
Proses: On Poems and Poets (Copper Canyon Press)

Denise Levertov (1923–1997) was born in England and was taught at home by her mother, never attending school except for five years of ballet, a Russian class, and a year of nursing school. Her mother read poetry to her from the time she was quite young. Levertov published her first poem, "Listening to Distant Guns," about the time of the Dunkirk evacuation, when she was seventeen, and her first book when she was twenty-three. The following year she married and then moved to America shortly after that. She joined the Black Mountain School of Poetry, which stressed the relationship between poetry and everyday life. In her writing, Levertov combined the personal, the spiritual, and the political, responding to the natural world, her religious beliefs, and such issues as the Vietnam War, the trial of Adolf Eichmann, and feminism.

Her last teaching position was at Stanford University, where she'd worked for many years. In an article about Levertov, her former student Anne-Marie Cusac wrote, "She had a disarming cackle, rode an old bicycle around campus, and wore skirts and practical shoes. . . . She did not lose arguments, even when she was probably wrong." In response to the Gulf War, Levertov, a peace activist for many years, organized students who carried Poets for Peace signs and marched in San Francisco with thousands of other citizens.

Levertov was the recipient of many prestigious awards— among them the Shelley Memorial Award, the Robert Frost Medal, and the Lenore Marshall Prize. She died at the age of seventy-four of cancer.

Suggested Reading:
Collected Earlier Poems, 1940–1960 (New Directions Press)

The Great Unknowing: Last Poems (New Directions Press)

Conversations with Denise Levertov (edited by Jewel Spears Brooker; Literary Conversation Series, University Press of Mississippi)

Philip Levine (b. 1928) was born in Detroit, Michigan, and attended Wayne State University, where he studied with some important poets of the century, including Robert Lowell. Levine is the author of sixteen books of poetry. He has also translated and edited poetry by Gloria Fuertes and Jaime Sabines. Levine teaches at Fresno State University and finds that teaching inspires his own writing. He has won numerous awards for his writing, most notably the Pulitzer Prize, the National Book Award, the American Book Award, and the Ruth Lilly Poetry Prize.

Suggested Reading:
  The Mercy (poems; Knopf)
  The Simple Truth (poems; Knopf)
  What Work Is (poems; Knopf)

Osip Mandelstam (1891–1938) was born in Warsaw to a middle-class Jewish family and grew up in St. Petersburg. He studied literature and philosophy in France and Germany. At first, his poetry did not center on politics, but as he got older he became more involved in the political climate of his time. In 1912 he became one of the Acmeist poets, along with Anna Akhmatova and Nikolai Gumilev. In 1921 he married Nadezhda Yakovlevna Khazina. They lived in Leningrad from 1924 to 1930, where he was under increasing pressure from the writers more favored than he. By 1934 publication was virtually impossible for him. During May of that year he was arrested, presumably because of a sardonic poem about Stalin that he had written but never published. His "counter-revolutionary activity" caused him great difficulty during his life; he was exiled more than once, attempted suicide, and then was held in a labor camp. The official date of his death was given as December 27, 1938, but there is doubt as to the accuracy of this. During his lifetime only three collections of his poetry were published, along with a few additional poems, some essays, autobiographical sketches, and a work of short fiction.

(Michael Henry Heim, professor of Slavic Languages and Literatures at UCLA, translated "Don't Tell a Soul" for this collection.)

Suggested Reading:
  Fifty Poems, 1946–1985 (Knopf)
  Selected Poems (translated by James Green; Viking Penguin)

Morton Marcus (b. 1936) is the author of eight books of poetry and one novel. His work has appeared in more than two hundred literary journals and seventy-five anthologies.

About his poem "The Girl Who Became My Grandmother," Marcus wrote, "Realistic art is the norm these days. We're instructed in creative writing classes to reproduce reality, copy nature. . . . But each scientific breakthrough tells us that what we experience through our senses is not reality, is not what's really going on. We're not solid matter. We're empty spaces composed of clusters of atoms spinning around each other . . . and we're regularly pierced by bits of blue light called neutrinos that fly through us to the ends of the universe. . . . What is truth, what lies? Does it matter if the girl/woman in my poem is really my grandmother? Does it matter that the kitchen in which she ran away became a coach . . . ? Or is my probing of the past what's important, the sense of magic still alive there that led to me, that leads to us all?"

Suggested Reading:

Moments Without Names (poems; New Rivers Press, forthcoming)

Pages from a Scrapbook of Immigrants: A Journey in Poems (Coffee House Press)

When People Could Fly (poems; Hanging Loose Press)

It is said that **James Merrill** (1926–1995) wrote poetry as a boy, producing a poem a day, and that he especially liked sonnets. He was born in New York City. He attended private schools and graduated from Lawrenceville in New Jersey. Merrill's mother was a significant force in his life. (He apparently kept a separate telephone with a number only she had.) When Merrill wrote a memoir called *A Different Person*, his mother discouraged him from publishing it, as she felt it to be too revealing of his homosexuality and of her anger over his "tendencies." Against her wishes, he published the book and in 1993 wrote her, saying, "I would have liked to abide by your wishes, but the impulse, the need to publish the memoir overcame my hesitation." In an article published in *Raritan*, his friend, the poet J. D. McClatchy, wrote that James Merrill "had a memory like no other I've encountered. In idle moments, he would purposefully call to mind rooms he had by chance been in years before. He'd imagine walking through each room, calling back to mind every piece of furniture in it, every object on its tables, and books on its shelves." Merrill's numerous awards include two National Book Awards, the Bollingen Prize, and the National Book Critics Circle Award.

Suggested Reading:
Selected Poems, 1946–1985 (Knopf)

W. S. Merwin (b. 1927) was born in New York City. In 1952 he was awarded a Yale Younger Poets Award. As a young man he worked as a tutor in many parts of the world, in France and Portugal and in Hawaii, where he lived for many years. Merwin is the author of more than fifteen books of poetry and translations, and four books of prose, including *The Lost Upland*, a memoir about his life in the south of France. In his most recent book, *The River Sound*, Merwin writes about his childhood, the lives and deaths of his parents, his marriage: "I am not certain as to how / the pain of learning what is lost / is transformed into light at last." But through his poems transformation does occur.

Suggested Reading:
Flower and Hand: Poems 1977–1983 (Copper Canyon Press)
The River Sound (poems; Knopf)
The Vixen (poems; Knopf)

Czeslaw Milosz (b. 1911) was born in Seteiniai, Lithuania. He went to high school and to the university in Wilno, which was then a part of Poland. In 1930 he cofounded the literary group Zagary and made his debut in literature shortly thereafter. Wartime forced Milosz, like many other artists in Poland, to work in hiding. He was involved in the underground presses. In 1951 he broke away from the government and settled in France. He was invited to the University of California at Berkeley to teach as professor of

Slavic Languages and Literatures. He received an honorary degree as a Doctor of Letters from the University of Michigan in 1977. Other awards and honors he has earned include a Guggenheim Fellowship for poetry in 1976 and a Berkeley Citation in 1978. Milosz won the Nobel Prize in Literature in 1980.

Suggested Reading:
  The Captive Mind (poems; Random House)
  Road-side Dog (Farrar, Straus & Giroux)

Merrill Moore (1903–1957) lived a dual professional life as both a poet and a psychiatrist. Born and raised in Tennessee, he later moved to Boston. His favorite poetic form was the sonnet, and he is said to have written fifty thousand of them. As a young man he belonged to a group of poets called The Fugitives that also included Laura Riding, Allen Tate, and Robert Penn Warren. The group published a magazine by the same name. He served in World War II as a psychiatrist, spending the greater part of the war in the Pacific. His medical writing includes such pieces as *War and Nerves* and *Alcoholism in Military Service.* Among his volumes of poetry are *Verse-Diary of a Psychiatrist* and *One Thousand Autobiographical Sonnets.*

Edith Nesbit's (1858–1924) father died when Edith was only six years old. Her mother, despite financial struggles, saw that her daughter received an education. When she was nineteen, Edith met and married a radical writer named Hubert Bland, with whom she became involved in the socialist politics of the day. They organized discussion groups and started a literary journal. A friend from the Fabian Society, as their group was called, lived with them for a while and ended up having a child by Hubert. Edith, apparently not jealous, took the baby into her care. Socialism was the main topic of her lectures and writings, until she became a successful children's book writer, publishing forty-four children's novels.

Suggested Reading:

Five Children and It (children's book; Viking Penguin)
The Railway Children (children's book; Penguin)

Before the Spanish conquest in Mexico, the region was ruled by kings. Although most of the rulers of the time were Aztecs, King **Nezahualcoyotl** (1403–1473) was of a tribe from the north, the Texcocans. Nezahualcoyotl was born heir to the throne, but when the Texcocans were invaded by Aztecs, his future looked pretty bleak. Yet the young man believed he had a right to the throne, and after escaping prison disguised as his servant, he went to the Aztec capital. The warm welcome he received there worried the ruling king, Maxtla, who ordered the prince to be killed. But Nezahualcoyotl managed to hide in a cave, and when enough people were fed up with their king, they revolted and replaced him with Nezahualcoyotl. He immediately became popular, setting down a code of laws based on a division of power. He encouraged art, literature, science, poetry, and history, and set up a system to verify the qualifications of professors, the accuracy of published works, and the patriotic and moral content of compositions. Nezahualcoyotl died at seventy, the father of 110 children.

Suggested Reading:

The Aztecs (by Michael E. Smith; Blackwell Publishers)
Flute of the Smoking Mirror: A Portrait of Nezahualcoyotl—Poet King of the Aztecs (by Frances Gillmor)

Currently a professor of fine art and of art history as well as the director of the Sankofa Center for the African Renaissance, **Pitika Ntuli** (b. 1942 in South Africa) has contributed poetry to numerous journals and anthologies. For ten years he has participated in Apples & Snakes Poetry, a weekly poetry performance circuit in London. Ntuli has performed his poems internationally.

Naomi Shihab Nye (b. 1952), born in St. Louis to an American mother and a Palestinian father, published her first poem at the age of seven. She has lived in Jerusalem and now makes her home in San Antonio, Texas. Place is a significant influence on her work. She says, "For me, the primary source of poetry has always been a local life, random characters met on the streets, our own ancestry sifting down to us through small essential daily tasks." Her poetry shows ordinary people, places, and events in a new light and reveals the similarities between and among people. Nye is the recipient of many awards, including four Pushcart Prizes, a Jane Addams Children's Book Award, the Patterson Poetry Prize, and many Notable Book and Best Book citations from the American Library Association.

Suggested Reading:
Different Ways to Pray (poems; BOA Editions)
Fuel (poems; BOA Editions)
Habibi (a novel for young people; Aladdin Paperbacks)
The Space Between Our Footsteps: Poems and Paintings from the Middle East (Simon & Schuster)

Kenneth Patchen (1911–1972) was born in Ohio. He started reading Shakespeare, Melville, Dante, and Homer at an early age. As a young man he had a variety of jobs. For more than thirty years, Patchen lived with a severe spinal ailment that caused him almost constant pain. His personal suffering deepened his awareness of the significant issues of humanity, peace, and war, and it influenced his poetry greatly. He wanted to provide a sanctuary for his reader, creating scenes and characters where people were motivated by benevolence and love.

Suggested Reading:
The Collected Poems of Kenneth Patchen (W. W. Norton)
What Shall We Do Without Us? (poem paintings; Sierra Club Books)

Octavio Paz (1914–1998) was born and raised in Mexico City, where he followed in his father's and his grandfather's footsteps and became politically active. He received a scholarship to study Hispanic poetry in the United States. During the Spanish Civil War, Paz, a sympathizer with the Republicans, went to Valencia, where he attended a conference of antifascist writers. When he returned to Mexico, he started a socialist-oriented magazine called *El Popular* and founded the publishing house Taller, which attracted new poets. In the 1950s he was the cultural attaché of Mexico in France. In addition to being a poet and a literary critic, Paz also wrote articles on the subject of visual art, dealing with Mexican painters, and Mexican pre-Hispanic art. Paz received many awards during his lifetime, including the Nobel Prize.

In 1997 an international news agency reported that Paz had died. Hearing this, he called a local television station and said, "The art of dying is the art of playing hide and seek, but you have to know how to play this part, which is then most delicate of all . . . and difficult."

Suggested Reading:
Collected Poems of Octavio Paz, 1957–1987 (New Directions Press)

Marge Piercy (b. 1936) has attracted many admirers for the political themes in her work. Like many other writers and artists, she was involved in the American civil rights movement of the 1960s and later became an active feminist. Her writing deals with issues of oppression, sexism, racism, poverty, and pollution. Nature also figures strongly. Although the realities her poems, essays, and novels illuminate are often harsh, she is ultimately optimistic about the potential for human beings to live together peacefully.

When asked why she's a poet, Piercy responded by saying, "What else should I be, like dead? Poetry is a necessity to me. Even when I have no access to paper or pen or silence, I make up poems. . . . I say poems to the peas and the day lilies. I make up poems for the houses on the street. . . . Those aren't meant to be great or public poems, just the little responses, the little grace notes of thanksgiving and praise."

Suggested Reading:
Available Light (poems; Knopf)
Mars and Her Children (poems; Knopf)

Sylvia Plath (1932–1963), from all outward appearances, seemed a happy child. She was popular, got straight A's, won all the school awards, and published her first poem at the age of eight. She received a scholarship to Smith College in 1950, by which point she had already published many poems. Below the surface, however, Plath's life was marked by a painful depression, which may have been caused by the death of her father when she was eight. She attempted suicide during her years at Smith but received treatment so that she graduated with highest honors and continued writing. After her marriage to poet Ted Hughes failed and she was living alone with her two children in a small London apartment, her depression returned. Many poems written during this time express a desire to die. She succeeded in killing herself at the age of thirty.

Suggested Reading:
The Collected Poems (HarperCollins)
The Bell Jar (a largely autobiographical novel; HarperCollins)

Ezra Pound (1885–1972) was well-traveled, well-read, and an extremely prolific and experimental writer. His work had an enormous effect on other modern writers such as W. B. Yeats, William Carlos Williams, Ernest Hemingway, James Joyce, H. D. (Hilda Doolittle), and T. S. Eliot. He incorporated thought from other cultures and religions, particularly those of the East, into his work. He is also known for his translations. Pound lived in various countries in Europe, eventually settling in Italy, where he became involved in fascist politics. In 1945 he was arrested for treason by the American government for broadcasting fascist propaganda in the United States. Eventually, after Pound spent time in a mental institution, the Bollingen–Library of Congress Award panel judges decided to overlook his political involvement and recognize his feats in poetry. In 1958 Pound returned to Italy, where he lived until his death in 1972.

Suggested Reading:

The Collected Early Poems of Ezra Pound (New Directions Press)

The Cantos (poems; New Directions Press)

Sir **Walter Ralegh** (c. 1554–1618) was a soldier, courtier, explorer, adventurer, historian, and poet whose life reads like a play. Born on a rented farm, he rose to become one of Queen Elizabeth's closest confidants and one of the leading men of his age. Yet each time it seemed he was about to reach the very highest ranks, he suffered a loss that nearly destroyed him—until he rose again. One of his biggest falls came when he secretly got a woman pregnant and then married her. When Elizabeth found out, she threw Ralegh and his wife in prison.

"The Lie" seems the kind of poem he could have written then, when all of his efforts to rise came crashing down. Still, scholars debate whether or not he actually wrote the poem, or if an enemy put his name to it in order to get him into trouble. Whoever wrote it, "The Lie" reveals aspects of Ralegh's personality: the clear-eyed cynic who saw through all the games he had to play at court, the devout man who passionately strove to succeed but also knew God would decide his fate. After one of the greatest trials in history, Ralegh was imprisoned for thirteen years. He was executed in 1618 after a last failed effort to find El Dorado.

(Ralegh's name is most often spelled Raleigh in America,

but that is not the way he usually wrote it. Though less familiar, the spelling used here is more accurate historically.)

Suggested Reading:
   Sir Walter Ralegh and the Quest for El Dorado (by Marc Aronson; Clarion)
   Sir Walter Ralegh (by Robert Lacey; Atheneum)

Poet, feminist, and political activist, **Adrienne Rich** (b. 1929) is a major figure in American letters. She is the author of nearly twenty books of poetry—most recently, *Midnight Salvage, Poems 1995–1998*—as well as four books of non-fiction prose. In 1999 she received the Lifetime Achievement Award from the Lannan Foundation. Previously, she has been awarded the Dorothea Tanning Prize and a MacArthur Fellowship. At twenty-one, she received the Yale Younger Poets Award. Hers is a brave, daring, and truth-telling poetry that addresses the strength of the human spirit. Her work demonstrates a belief in the power of poetry. Rich wrote, "The necessity of poetry has to be stated over and over to those who have reason to fear its power, those who still believe that language is only words and that any old language is good enough for our description of the world we are trying to transform."

Suggested Reading:
   The Dream of a Common Language (W. W. Norton)
   Midnight Salvage: Poems 1995–1998 (W. W. Norton)
   On Lies, Secrets and Silence: Selected Prose 1966–1978 (W. W. Norton)

Little that is definitive is known about the poet **Sappho**, who lived around 600 B.C.E. on the Greek island of Lesbos. The oldest surviving biographical material about her was written several centuries after she died. Traveling to Lesbos in 1985, Patrice Vecchione found few signs of her having lived there: only two statues on the entire island, not much attention for a poet who has had international stature for centuries.

   Though most of Sappho's poetry has come to us in

fragments, which scholars have had to reassemble, she is regarded as a remarkable poet. Plato, among others, considered her the tenth Muse. She wrote first-person poetry about desire and love as well as the natural world. She is considered the first poet ever to refer to the moon as "silver," and she was praised for this. Her work displays a lack of self-consciousness and a love for women. During Sappho's time, poetry was sung or recited to musical accompaniment before audiences. She was one of the first poets known for a new style of poetry, a type of lyric poetry called the monodic, sung by a single voice.

Suggested Reading:

Sappho: A New Translation by Mary Barnard (University of California Press)

William Shakespeare (c. 1564–1616) is the world's most famous and respected playwright. He was born in Warwickshire, England, to middle-class parents as the third child and first son of eight children. His father worked with leather goods and was a dealer in agricultural commodities, a man on the rise, serving as a member of the town council in Stratford. We can probably assume that Shakespeare went to school and studied the classical texts, since his father had an important position in society and children of prominent figures were educated. His plays were performed in the Globe Theatre, where people of all different classes would come and sit on different tiers of the playhouse to see his work performed. Shakespeare was a master at creating plays that could be understood and appreciated on multiple levels.

There are many people who insist that Shakespeare was, in fact, not the true author of the work credited to his name because there is little evidence that links the man named Shakespeare to the works he produced. Joseph Sobran, the author of *Alias Shakespeare*, believes, like many scholars, that the man who actually wrote what is credited to

Shakespeare was Edward de Vere, the seventeenth earl of Oxford.

Suggested Reading:
  Complete Poems of Shakespeare (Random House)
  Complete Works of William Shakespeare (Library of Congress Classic)

Gertrude Stein (1874–1946) lived on the cutting edge of the literary and art world of her day. She was born in Vienna, raised in California, and after studying psychology with William James at Radcliffe College and attending Johns Hopkins medical school, she went to Paris, where she was able to live by private means. She collected art by Picasso (who painted her portrait) and other experimental painters and mingled in her salon with Ernest Hemingway, Henri Matisse, and Georges Braque. Her writing reflects the ideas of her Cubist friends, using methods of abstraction and fragmentation to illuminate the present. Stein survived the German occupation of France and befriended many young American servicemen who visited her. From 1912 until her death in 1946, Gertrude Stein lived with the love of her life, Alice B. Toklas.

Suggested Reading:
  Tender Buttons (poems; Dover)
  Three Lives (fiction; Dover)
  The Autobiography of Alice B. Toklas (a memoir; Random House)

Anne Stevenson (b. 1933) is an American who was born in England. She was educated at the University of Michigan and returned to England to marry; she has lived there ever since, though she still considers herself to be American. She says, "I have had a mixed life as a wife, mother, school teacher, and writer in residence." She's the author of twelve books of poetry, a biography of Sylvia Plath, and two books about Elizabeth Bishop, as well as a book of essays.

The translation of the title of her poem that appears here, "Sous-Entendu," means "hidden meaning" or "implication." Stevenson wrote, "In one sense it [hidden meaning] does lie at the heart of my work, for throughout my writing (and real) life I have been constantly at pains to distinguish (emotional) truths from lies. . . . [I]t seems to me that literature, poetry and fiction, is obliged to explore psychological and emotional distinctions that are left out or buried under the public veneer. Poetry should use public language to describe private truths, however uncomfortable and self-contradictory."

Suggested Reading:
  Collected Poems, 1955–1995 (Oxford University Press)
  Granny Scarecrow (poems; Bloodaxe Books)
  Between the Iceberg and the Ship (essays; University of Michigan Press)

The Navajo poet **Torlino** was sent to Carlisle Industrial Indian School in Pennsylvania by his father, Old Torlino, a priest of *hozóni hatál* (the Blessing Way). When he returned, according to Washington Matthews in *Navaho Legends*, published in 1897, "The writer sent for the old man to get from him the myth of *hozóni hatál*. Old Torlino began: 'I know the white men say the world is round, and that it floats in the air. My tale says the world is flat, and that there are five worlds, one above another. You will not believe my tale, then, and perhaps you do not want to hear it.' Being assured that the tale was earnestly desired, he proceeded. 'I shall tell you the truth, then. I shall tell you all that I heard from the old men who taught me, as well as I can now remember. Why should I lie to you?' "

Suggested Reading:
  Navajo: Visions and Voices Across the Mesa (by Shonto Begay; Scholastic, Inc.)
  Storm Pattern: Poems from Two Navajo Women (by Della Frank with Roberta D. Joe; Dine College Press)

Margaret Walker (1915–1998) was a poet, novelist, and essayist who began writing during the Harlem Renaissance. She was born in Birmingham, Alabama, and lived in the Jim Crow South, of which she said in a 1940s interview, "Before I was ten, I knew what it was to step off the sidewalk to let a white man pass; otherwise he might knock me off." She was awarded the Yale Series of Younger Poets Award. For many years she lived in Jackson, Mississippi, where she was a professor emeritus of English and the director of the Institute for the Study of History, Life and Culture of Black Peoples at Jackson State College.

Suggested Reading:
   On Being Female, Black and Free: Essays, 1932–1992 (University of Tennessee Press)
   This Is My Century: New and Collected Poems (University of Georgia Press)

Bruce Weigl (b. 1949) was born in Lorain, Ohio, and is the author of ten collections of poetry and the editor of three collections of critical essays. Many of his poems portray the trauma and reality of war. He speaks of flesh and spirit, violence and sex, love and loneliness. His poetry and translations have appeared in many important journals and anthologies and have been recognized with awards, including the Pushcart Prize, the Patterson Poetry Prize, a prize from the American Academy of Poets, a Yaddo Foundation Fellowship, and a National Endowment for the Arts Grant for Poetry.

Suggested Reading:
   Song of Napalm (poems; Grove Atlantic)
   What Saves Us (poems; Northwestern University Press)

William Carlos Williams (1883–1963), like Chekhov, was a country doctor before he was a writer, although he enjoyed writing poetry since he was a child. He was born and raised in New Jersey and received his M.D. from the University of Pennsylvania. At the university he met and befriended

Ezra Pound, who was to become a big influence on his writing. Williams started writing for journals while he was practicing medicine and continued to pursue the two professions for the rest of his life. He is known for his common language and subjects and for the belief that ideas are not in words but in the things themselves. About poetry Williams said, "It is difficult / to get the news from poems / yet men die miserably every day / for lack / of what is found there." He impressed the Beats, the group of writers including Jack Kerouac and Allen Ginsberg who were part of the rebellious artistic movement of the late 1940s through 1960s, with his accessibility and his openness as a mentor. Despite declining health, Williams continued to work up until his death in New Jersey in 1963.

Suggested Reading:

The Collected Poems of William Carlos Williams (New Directions Press)

The Collected Short Stories of William Carlos Williams (New Directions Press)

The Autobiography of William Carlos Williams (W. W. Norton)

The Letters of Denise Levertov and William Carlos Williams (New Directions Press)

Janet S. Wong (b. 1962) was born in Los Angeles and grew up in California. At the University of California at Los Angeles, she founded the Immigrant Children's Art Project, and received her B.A. She received her law degree from Yale Law School and practiced corporate and labor law for a few years but then decided that she was more interested in writing books for young people. Many of her poems have appeared in textbooks and anthologies—and in some more unusual places, including on five thousand posters that were displayed in subway trains and buses as part of the New York Metropolitan Transit Authority's Poetry in Motion program. She's the recipient of many awards, including the

International Reading Association's Celebrate Literacy Award, presented by the Foothill Reading Council.

Suggested Reading:
A Suitcase of Seaweed: And Other Poems (Simon & Schuster)
The Trip Back Home (poems; Harcourt Brace)

Rita Wong's (b. 1968) first book of poems, *monkeypuzzle*, won the Asian Canadian Writers Workshop Emerging Writing Award in 1998 and was a finalist for the Lambda Literary Award for Poetry. She grew up in Calgary and is currently living in Vancouver. Wong has worked as an archivist, an English teacher in China and Japan, and a coordinator for the Alberta/Northwest Territories Network of Immigrant Women. Her writing has been published in many journals and anthologies, and her poems have appeared on buses and trains as part of the Poetry in Transit projects in Toronto and Vancouver.

Suggested Reading:
monkeypuzzle (Press Gang Publishers)

William Butler Yeats (1865–1939) was an Irish Nationalist, known for his spirit and attachment to Irish traditions. His early poetry drew upon Irish legend and myth, but his later poetry focused on the Ireland of his day and his reactions to it. Yeats was born in Dublin and lived in London for the majority of his life. In 1889 he fell in love with Maud Gonne who never returned his feelings. He wrote plays as well as poetry and founded the Irish National Theatre Society, which later became the Abbey Theatre. He was described as a "lank, dark-coated figure who came and went as he pleased," who "dramatized himself in the streets of London" and later criticized political leaders freely. Yeats wanted to use his art to make people more aware of what was going on around them; he wanted to transform not only language but the world.

Suggested Reading:
Collected Poems of W. B. Yeats (Scribner)
Fairy and Folk Tales of Ireland (edited by W. B. Yeats; Simon & Schuster)

Yevgeny Yevtushenko (b. 1933) was a post-Stalin Russian poet who showed a loyalty to communism in many of his early poems, then became a leader for the young post-Stalinist generation. Yevtushenko was of the fourth generation of Ukrainians exiled to Siberia. He moved to Moscow in 1944 where he studied at the Gorky Institute of Literature. Yevtushenko's poetry demands greater freedom for artists and a break from the Nazism, anti-Semitism, and bureaucracy that had been part of the Stalinist government. In the '50s and '60s, he became a leader of Soviet youth and traveled often in the West. Active in many societies, he continues to urge political reform and awareness.

Suggested Reading:
The Collected Poems, 1952–1990 (Henry Holt)

PERMISSIONS

Permission for use of the following is gratefully acknowledged:

INDEX OF AUTHORS

Alvarez, Julia, 13, 61–62, 97
Amichai, Yehuda, 31, 97–98
Anonymous, 84, 104
Arnett, Carroll/Gogisgi, 20, 107
Atwood, Margaret, 25–26,
    98–99

Blake, William, 35, 99
Brecht, Bertolt, 56–57, 99–100
Bukowski, Charles, 95, 100
Burgos, Julia de, 44–45,
    100–101
Burns, Diane, 47–48, 101
Butler, Samuel, 78, 101

Carson, Jo, 76–77, 101–2
Carver, Raymond, 63, 102
Chekhov, Anton, 63, 102–3
Clarke, Cheryl, 37, 103
Clifton, Lucille, 14, 103–4
Crane, Stephen, 27, 104
Crow people, 9, 105

Davis, Cortney, 42–43, 105–6
Dickinson, Emily, 40, 106

Etherege, Sir George, 85, 106

Gensler, Kinereth, 51, 106–7
Gogisgi/Carroll Arnett, 20, 107

Hall, Donald, 58, 107–8
Harizi, Juda al-, 73, 108

Harjo, Joy, 12, 108–9
Herbert, Zbigniew, 59–60,
    89–90, 109
Herrick, Robert, 21, 22,
    109–10
Hill, Jonell, 17–19, 110
Hogan, Linda, 53–54, 110

Ignatow, David, 72, 111

Jiménez, Juan Ramón, 46,
    111–12
Jones, Rodney, 34, 112

Kabir, 88, 112
Kay, Jackie, 32–33, 112–13
Kipling, Rudyard, 93, 113
Kizer, Carolyn, 74, 113–14

Levertov, Denise, 7–8, 114–15
Levine, Philip, 3, 115–16

Mandelstam, Osip, 52, 116
Marcus, Morton, 91–92,
    116–17
Merrill, James, 70, 117–18
Merwin, W. S., 5–6, 118
Milosz, Czeslaw, 49–50,
    118–19
Moore, Merrill, 71, 119

Nesbit, Edith, 69, 119–20
Nezahualcoyotl, King, 94, 120

Ntuli, Pitika, 55, 120
Nye, Naomi Shihab, 28, 121

Patchen, Kenneth, 10–11, 121
Paz, Octavio, 4, 122
Piercy, Marge, 36, 122–23
Plath, Sylvia, 41, 123
Pound, Ezra, 75, 123–24

Ralegh, Sir Walter, 80–83,
    124–25
Rich, Adrienne, 64–65, 125

Sappho, 67, 125–26
Shakespeare, William, 66,
    126–27

Stein, Gertrude, 16, 127
Stevenson, Anne, 79, 127–28

Torlino, 29, 128

Walker, Margaret, 23–24, 129
Weigl, Bruce, 38–39, 129
Williams, William Carlos, 86,
    129–30
Wong, Janet S., 30, 130–31
Wong, Rita, 68, 131
Wu-ti, Emperor, 74

Yeats, William Butler, 87,
    131–32
Yevtushenko, Yevgeny, 15, 132

INDEX OF TITLES

"And the days are not full enough" (Pound), 75
"Appeal" (Nesbit), 69

"Beat" (Wong), 30
"Be Like Others" (Milosz), 49–50
"Bilingual Sestina" (Alvarez), 61–62
"Body Politic, The" (Hall), 58
"Box Called the Imagination, A" (Herbert), 89–90
"Brotherhood" (Paz), 4

"Cartographies of Silence" (Rich), 64–65
"Caught" (Jones), 34
"Clay Jug, The" (Kabir), 88
"Come All You Fair and Tender Ladies" (Anonymous), 84
"crush" (Wong), 68

"Democratic Judge, The" (Brecht), 56–57
"Denial" (Gensler), 51
"Don't Tell a Soul" (Mandelstam), 52

"Fool's Song, The" (Williams), 86
"Four Masks" (Davis), 42–43
"Fragment 26" (Sappho), 67

"Girl Who Became My Grandmother, The" (Marcus), 91–92

"Hiding Our Love" (Kizer), 74
"Horse's Head" (Hill), 17–19
"How She Resolved to Act" (Moore), 71
"Hypocrisy" (Butler), 78

"I Am Asking You to Come Back Home" (Carson), 76–77
"I Am Not I" (Jiménez), 46
"In My Country" (Ntuli), 55

"Lie, The" (Ralegh), 80–83
"Lies" (Yevtushenko), 15

"Mirror" (Plath), 41

"no help for that" (Bukowski), 95
"Not Forever on Earth" (Nezahualcoyotl), 94

"Old Man Said: One, The" (Gogisgi/Carroll Arnett), 20
"Other Voices, The" (Hogan), 53–54
"Our Lies and Their Beauty" (Weigl), 38–39
"Our Principal" (Nye), 28

"Poison Tree, A" (Blake), 35

"Remember" (Harjo), 12
"Renewal, A" (Merrill), 70

"Secret, The" (Levertov), 7–8
"Secret Kept, A" (al-Harizi), 73
"Shadow Play for Guilt, A" (Piercy), 36
"Simple Truth, The" (Levine), 3
"Small Heart" (Herbert), 59–60
"Smoke and Deception" (Carver), 63
"Song" (Etherege), 85
"Song of Lies on Sabbath Eve, A" (Amichai), 31
"Song of the Bald Eagle" (Crow People), 9
"Sous-Entendu" (Stevenson), 79
"Stincher, The" (Kay), 32–33
"Sure You Can Ask Me a Personal Question" (Burns), 47–48

"teachers taught her that the world was round, The" (Stein), 16
"Tell All the Truth" (Dickinson), 40

"Therefore I Must Tell the Truth" (Torlino), 29
"33" (Alvarez), 13
"To a Friend Whose Work Has Come to Nothing" (Yeats), 87
"To Julia de Burgos" (de Burgos), 44–45
"True Stories" (Atwood), 25–26
"Truth" (Herrick), 22
"Truth and Falsehood" (Herrick), 21

"Unwritten, The" (Merwin), 5–6

"Wayfarer, The" (Crane), 27
"Way Through the Woods, The" (Kipling), 93
"We Have Been Believers" (Walker), 23–24
"what goes around comes around or the proof is in the pudding" (Clarke), 37
"When my love swears that she is made of truth" (Shakespeare), 66
"When We Were Here Together" (Patchen), 10–11
"why some people be mad at me sometimes" (Clifton), 14
"With the Door Open" (Ignatow), 72